Sherlock Holmes

and

The Shadows of St Petersburg

[Being another manuscript found in the dispatch box of
Dr. John H. Watson
In the vault of Cox & Co., Charing Cross, London]

As Edited

By

Daniel D. Victor, Ph.D.

Paperback ISBN 978-1-78705-288-8
ePub ISBN 978-1-78705-289-5
PDF ISBN 978-1-78705-290-1

Published in the UK by MX Publishing
335 Princess Park Manor, Royal Drive
London, N11 3GX
www.mxpublishing.co.uk
Cover design by Brian Belanger

Also by Daniel D. Victor

The Seventh Bullet:
The Further Adventures of Sherlock Holmes

A Study in Synchronicity

The Final Page of Baker Street
(Book One in the series,
Sherlock Holmes and the American Literati)

Sherlock Holmes and the Baron of Brede Place
(Book Two in the series,
Sherlock Holmes and the American Literati)

Seventeen Minutes to Baker Street
(Book Three in the series,
Sherlock Holmes and the American Literati)

The Outrage at the Diogenes Club
(Book Four in the series,
Sherlock Holmes and the American Literati)

Here's another for Norma, Seth and Ethan.

Acknowledgments

For their consistent help and encouragement, I'd like to thank Norma Silverman, Judy Grabiner, Barry Smolin, Sandy Cohen, David Marcum, and Mark Holzband. A special thanks to Seth Victor for his tech-help and to Ethan Victor for sharing his writing time with me.

A hundred suspicions don't make a proof.

Nothing in the world is harder than speaking the truth,
and nothing easier than flattery.

Man grows used to everything, the scoundrel!

--Fyodor Dostoevsky
Crime and Punishment
Constance Garnett Translation

A Note on the Text

Footnotes followed by (JHW) were included by Dr Watson in the original manuscript. Footnotes followed by (DDV) were added by the editor.

Prologue

"The bullet wound suffered by Mr Arthur Black was not sufficient to kill him." Thus spoke the Deputy Coroner for East Sussex on a January day in 1893. What exactly had ended the man's life was yet to be acknowledged.

At the time of the inquest, close to two years following the supposedly fatal encounter between Sherlock Holmes and Professor Moriarty at the Reichenbach Falls, the general public (myself included) still believed Holmes to be dead. And yet— as I have noted elsewhere—in spite of his disappearance, I never lost interest in the challenges of forensic medicine that my friend had kindled within me.

As a result, I continued to follow public reports of crimes and their ensuing investigations during Holmes' absence. Indeed, owing to my familiarity with the official police force, I would not infrequently be asked for my medical opinion on various criminal matters. When the Scotland

Yarders said, "Dr Watson, your services are required," I did my best to oblige. Even without the guidance of my trusted friend, I should like to think that I made more than a few worthwhile contributions to their cases.[1]

As a consequence of my willingness to represent the Yard beyond the boundaries of London, it came as no surprise when in early 1893 I was invited to testify at a public inquest in Brighton. Though I am certain a local doctor could have done the work just as effectively, I assumed that police officials, desirous of keeping controversy to a minimum, hoped the appearance at the inquest of a colleague of the late Sherlock Holmes might add credibility to a singular murder investigation.

One can always count on the public's ghoulish fascination with murder, a fascination that grows with the number of victims and multiplies exponentially if the dead happen to be personages of distinction. In the Brighton business, there were three dead. But in this case, it was not the usual gawkers that concerned themselves with the morbid

----

[1] For exploration of my police work following Holmes' retirement, see *The Outrage at the Diogenes Club*. (JHW)

details; it was a group of influential intellectuals that displayed keen interest in an explanation for the multiple murders.

As it happened, one of the deceased, the aforementioned Arthur Black, was a recognised mathematician. He also happened to be the brother-in-law of noted author and critic Edward Garnett, whose father Richard served as Keeper of the Printed Books at the British Museum. Though Edward's wife Constance, the sister of the dead man, had not yet begun her celebrated translations of Russian literature, she had already completed studies in Greek and Latin at Cambridge. With so much of the intelligentsia displaying interest, the Yard concluded that the criminal investigation needed to be treated with particular care.

*****

The facts in the case were these: On Tuesday, 17 January, 1893, Mr Black, a teacher of mathematics at the School of Science and Art in Brighton, failed to appear for his first class of the new term. After two days of receiving no response to written queries, the school secretary took it upon himself to visit the teacher's home at 27 Goldstone Villas.

When he received no answer to his persistent knocks, he notified the local constabulary.

It was Detective Walter Parsons who responded to the secretary's concern. Parsons, accompanied by Ernest Black, Arthur's brother, gained entrance to the lower level of the teacher's house by breaking a garden window. Later, in a detail deemed irrelevant by the authorities at the inquest, it was noted that at the time of their entry a door to the garden had been unbolted.

Whatever the two men had overlooked in their haste to enter, they would not soon forget the horrors they encountered once they got inside. As described by the detective, first they came upon the lifeless body of Arthur's infant son. Dressed in nightclothes, the baby lay in a pool of blood. There was a knife wound to the back of the neck, and the skull had been crushed.

Next, they found the body of Black's wife. She was lying on her back, a pool of brain matter and blood having formed beneath her head. Nearby, a trail of blood led to the staircase. It was upstairs in the couple's bedroom that the two men discovered the dead body of the missing teacher. Dressed in his nightshirt and lying face downward on the bed, Arthur

Black had bled heavily from the nose. The non-lethal bullet wound described at the start of this narrative was located in his right thigh.

On the table next to Arthur's body, Parsons noted a revolver, the kind the Americans call a "six-shooter". Four of its six bullets had been fired. Also on the table were a blood-stained hammer, a knife, and a group of medicine bottles containing chloroform.

Upon examining Black's body, Edward Treves, the police surgeon, posited that a deranged Arthur Black, after murdering his wife and child, had killed himself by drinking the sweet-smelling liquid. Such a desperate act, Treves said, would explain the excessive bleeding from Black's nose as well as the observation by a neighbour that earlier in the day of the killings Arthur had looked "wild". Nothing accounted for the bullet wound in the man's thigh.

The authorities concluded that Black had been insane when he performed these murderous acts, but it seemed to me that testimony critical of his wife raised questions about her own possible involvement in the matter. Witnesses considered Jesse Black a drunk, a misfit, a liar—in short, a woman of ill repute. She had been delusional, they said, overheard by

13

neighbours on at least one occasion screaming out that she was being strangled when, in fact, she was not.

Adding to the confusion, one witness reported having heard no more than two shots fired—certainly not four—on the night of the murder and no multiple screams. Another witness testified to having seen Arthur Black in the street well after the police surgeon believed him to have died. And there still remained the curious matter of the door that had remained unbolted. I fancied how the inquest's ignoring of that clue would have irked Sherlock Holmes.

"Surely," I argued with Detective Parsons, "the unbolted door suggests the possibility that someone else might have perpetrated these horrific acts. Such a villain could easily have made his escape through the garden door. With no key in his possession, he would have been unable to lock the door from the outside, and it would have remained unlocked in precisely the condition in which it was found."

Absent any credible proof of such possibilities, however, the police appeared more than satisfied with Mr Treves' original premise—that mother and child had been murdered by Mr Black who went on to drink the chloroform and kill himself.

In the end, possessing no reasonable alternatives to offer the jury, I could muster little conviction in my argument to them for prolonging the investigation: "Gentlemen," I pleaded, "there is no need to rush to judgement. There may yet be other explanations to examine before a correct conclusion can be reached with any degree of certainty."

Oh, that the jury disregarded my plea did not surprise me. Yet I cannot rid myself of the notion that had Sherlock Holmes been involved, any undiscovered facts would most certainly have been brought to light. What is more, I believe that the Garnett family clearly agreed with my suspicions. Why else would Richard Garnett, writing in his biography of his grandmother Constance, lament the absence of my missing friend? With so much of the case sounding "like the language of Sherlock Holmes," he observed, "one almost expects the great detective to take over and explain all."[2]

Alas, no such saviour was forthcoming; and in response to the decisive but unconvincing verdict—that "mother and child came to their death by the hand of Mr Black and that Mr Black destroyed himself whilst of unsound mind"—the family chose to sweep the entire matter under the proverbial carpet.

---

[2] *Constance Garnett: A Heroic Life* (DDV)

*****

So marked my initial involvement with the Garnett family. A second meeting took place in early 1899. Some five years after Holmes had returned to Baker Street from his putative death, we found ourselves in pursuit of a master blackmailer. One of his victims was the American novelist Stephen Crane, then living in England.[3]

Now it should be noted that one could not enter into Crane's orbit without also bumping into various members of his literary circle. Writers like Joseph Conrad, Ford Madox Ford, HG Wells, Henry James, and—more to the point—Edward and Constance Garnett were frequent visitors to Crane's home.

The Garnetts happened to live close by the Cranes just southeast of London in Surrey. Indeed, the Cearne, the Garnetts' newly built stone-and-oak house in Limpsfield Chart, stood only a few miles from Ravensbrook, the Cranes'

---

[3] Details of the blackmail case may be found in my account titled *Sherlock Holmes and the Baron of Brede Place* (JHW)

unassuming brick villa in Oxted, which Edward had suggested they rent.

Holmes and I had occasion to stop at Ravensbrook during our investigation into the blackmail entanglement. Months later, once the Cranes had moved to their stately—albeit rundown—mansion called Brede Place (another home recommended to them by Edward), the Garnetts joined many other celebrated guests at the *soirées* the Cranes hosted there. In fact, Constance's brother-in-law, architect Harry Cowlishaw, was said to have provided a number of recommendations for improving the once-grand manor house.

Like Brede Place, the Cearne also attracted its share of serious writers. Over the years, literary figures like Galsworthy and Lawrence would join the crowd that had frequented Brede Place. My opportunity came in late 1899, when our investigation on behalf of Stephen Crane provided me the chance opportunity to meet the Garnetts.

Not long thereafter, I was honoured to receive an invitation to one of the Garnetts' social gatherings, an especially treasured invitation since it was tendered to me in my capacity as author rather than amateur sleuth. Apparently, I had established some sort of reputation for myself.

In truth, in the years following the publication of *A Study in Scarlet*, I produced more than twenty sketches for *The Strand* concerning my adventures with Sherlock Holmes. Who would have thought that as a result of recording our various investigations, that I, John H. Watson in the spring of 1900, would find myself at the Cearne joining the literati for tea and biscuits? But there I was, discussing not only the most vexing of literary questions, but also the latest political developments facing Europe—especially the social unrest in Russia.

I enjoyed my time with the Garnetts. Edward had made a name for himself in the field of literary analysis, and his efforts to popularise Crane's work in particular are well known. Yet I was particularly charmed by Edward's soft-spoken, bespectacled wife some ten years my junior.

Constance Garnett's studies at Cambridge spoke well of her intellectual prowess. In spite of her distinguished education, however, I should judge that in the late '90s only the most discerning of readers would have recognised her name. Today, of course, her numerous English translations of Russian works demonstrate just how talented a linguist she is.

Inspired by an assortment of Russian *émigrés* in England, Mrs Garnett first travelled to Russia not long after her brother's alleged suicide. Eager to practice Russian and enchanted by the writings of Turgenev, she decided to translate them into English, an undertaking that garnered much approval from the literary world. Buoyed by her early success, she set her mind on translating additional authors like Tolstoy, Gontcharoff, and Ostrovsky as well.

But not, alas, Fyodor Dostoevsky. In spite of her growing familiarity with the works of many important Russian writers, Mrs Garnett was initially steered away from his writings. Her publisher William Heinemann (who also produced many of Crane's works) suspected that what he called a British "fear of morbidity" would dampen any public interest in Dostoevsky's tenebrous novels. To put it more cynically, one may assume that Heinemann worried such translations would fail to generate substantial profits.

Enter John Watson. In April of '05 I had the good fortune to be invited by Mrs Garnett to a gathering of writers she convened at her flat in Hampstead. Though the get-together turned out to be the last time I have seen her, I believe it to have been a seminal event.

In addressing a hostess known for her familiarity with Russian texts, it seemed only natural to relate to her the details of a crime Holmes investigated that mirrored the events in a Russian novel. I refer, of course, to the case involving a pair of horrific axe-killings in London's East End in the fall of '87.

Though it is only now that I make the narrative public, no one familiar with *Crime and Punishment*—Dostoevsky's fictional account of two cold-blooded murders committed in St Petersburg, Russia, some twenty years before the London killings—could fail to note the similarities.

Indeed, I am pleased to report that Mrs Garnett sat spellbound for the duration of my account of the grim affair, and it is that same story which follows this prologue. Humility prohibits me from advertising my own importance in the matter; and yet I must point out that it was not long after I had related the events to Mrs Garnett that she began producing her own English versions of Dostoevsky's major writings, *Crime and Punishment* among them.

To be sure, others had attempted translating the works of Dostoevsky before she undertook the role. By way of example, one may cite Marie von Thilo's treatment of *Buried Alive* or Frederick Whishaw's translation of *The Idiot*. But as those editions earned little popular acclaim, I consider it no exaggeration to state that, owing to the clarity and precision of her expressive prose, it is to Constance Garnett alone that we should pay homage for introducing Dostoevsky to the English-speaking world.

I would like to believe that the gruesome tale I related that evening in 1905 helped stimulate Mrs Garnett's productivity. Trusting that it did enables me to view its publication as a form of atonement, a kind of compensation, if you will, for my inability at the inquest in '93 to fully explain what had happened to Arthur Black and his family.

At the very least, such thinking allows me to regard Mrs Garnett's success in translating the world of Russian thought into English as antidote to the guilt that has pursued me all these years. At long last, I may now finally be able to lay the matter to rest.

John H. Watson, M.D.

London, June 1927

Chapter One

In Quintum Novembris
(On the Fifth of November)
--John Milton

"A double murder," announced Lestrade on a cold Tuesday morning in late '87.

Like a magical incantation, the words of the policeman served to excite the passions of Sherlock Holmes. My friend extinguished the flame he had just caused to erupt from his Bunsen burner and stood upright. "Pray, take a chair," said he to Lestrade, "and give us the details."

It may seem obvious to begin the account of the gruesome double axe-murders with the arrival of the police inspector. But such a strategy belies the true origin of the matter. An earlier occurrence in the last week of October—just after our business with Henry James had concluded[4] and just a few days before the start of the case I titled "The Red Headed League"—was equally important in shaping the course of our investigation into the brutal murders. Maybe even more so. I simply did not comprehend its significance at the time.

In the years following my return from military service, I made it my business toward the end of each October to stop in at the London Library in St James's Square. In such a fashion, I anticipated the arrival of the riotous Guy Fawkes Day festivities, the annual celebrations that commemorate the foiling of the Gun Powder Plot, the treacherous scheme in November of 1605, which sought to destroy the entire British government.

Soothing my nerves remained a necessity in those early years back from Afghanistan, and thus I established the habit of securing new reading material to prepare for the riotous holiday. Escaping between the covers of an engaging book never failed to deaden the maddening shrieks and wild chants of the madcap revellers running amok in Baker Street. After

---

[4] See "The Adventure of the Aspen Papers" in *The MX Book of New Sherlock Holmes Stories, Part I*, edited by David Marcum. (DDV)

all, how many times can one tolerate the old nursery rhyme: "Remember, remember! The Fifth of November"?

It was not as if I had no other distractions—at least, not in the fall of '87. Why, in less than three weeks—on the twenty-first—my very first Holmes narrative, *A Study in Scarlet*, was set to appear in print. And yet not even my excitement over its upcoming publication in *Beeton's Christmas Annual* could deter my intention during Guy Fawkes Day to travel on my own in the diverting literary landscape of some other author.

My friend Lomax, the sub-librarian at the London Library, knew my tastes. Not only had he become acquainted with my late-October desires, but he also appreciated my *penchant* for the latest books on crime. Greeting me with a conspiratorial grin, therefore, he whispered, "I have something for you, Watson," and reaching below the red mahogany countertop, withdrew a substantial-looking volume with burgundy boards. "It's a Russian novel about a pair of hatchet murders," he said softly.

I took the book and examined the title page: *Crime and Punishment* by Fyodor Dostoevsky. I had not heard of the work, and I knew nothing of its author save that his name sounded Russian.

"It was written more than twenty years ago," Lomax explained, "but Dostoevsky died recently, and just last year Whishaw translated it into English."

I did know of Fred Whishaw, the popular English novelist. He had been born in St Petersburg, and one could assume a competent translation. I thanked Lomax for his help and with my new treasure in hand marched off to Baker Street more confident than ever of avoiding the distraction of the upcoming revelry.

Happily, the Saturday that was the Fifth of November came and went without any major disruptions. My thick Russian novel had successfully fulfilled its purpose. So engaging was the book, in fact, that on the following Tuesday morning I sat before the spluttering log fire finishing its final pages.

At the same time, Sherlock Holmes, dressed in shirtsleeves, was in the midst of setting up his Bunsen burner. He appeared to be in preparation of bringing some vile-smelling liquid to a boil when, just as I was completing the last page, we were interrupted by a knock on the door.

"Yes?" I answered.

Billy, our boy in buttons, entered to announce, "Inspector Lestrade." Straightening his tunic and standing even taller, he added, "Of Scotland Yard."

The lad had scarcely completed his pronouncement when in strode the man himself. Dressed to face the elements, Lestrade sported a bowler atop his head, a scarf round his neck, and a full-length, heavy coat enveloping his frame.

Still clutching my Russian novel, I rose to greet him. Holmes, however, continued fidgeting with the burner.

To give Lestrade his due, he knew how to capture my friend's attention. Waving with limp hand at the flame over which Holmes was hovering, the Inspector said, "If you can bring yourself to break away from whatever fiddle-faddle you're up to, Mr Holmes, I have a case that I thought might interest you."

"A case, you say?"

"That's right," said the policeman with a sardonic grin. It was then that he dangled the bait to which I referred at the start of this narrative. "I speak of a double murder."

Eyes alight, Holmes gestured for the man to remove his coat, and Lestrade hung it along with his hat and scarf upon the pegs near the door. Rubbing his hands together, he eagerly approached our hearth.

"What has happened?" I asked as the three of us settled in before the fire.

"Ordinarily, gentlemen, I wouldn't waste your morning with a murder case in the East End. Routine business, usually."

We could all attest to the human misery in that part of the great metropolis—the lack of food, the lack of heat, the lack of work. It was just such conditions that caused the respectable classes to avoid the danger and violence permeating the area. And yet it would require almost two decades to pass before Jack London, the American writer who started us off on that business concerning the Assassination Bureau, would describe the poor souls who lived in the East End as "people of the abyss".[5]

"A Jewish pawnbroker called Gottfried was killed yesterday evening a bit after 7.," Lestrade offered matter-of-factly. "Quite a religious fellow, I'm told."

---

[5] See my aforementioned narrative entitled *The Outrage at the Diogenes Club*. (JHW)

"Any victim of murder deserves justice," Holmes intoned. "His religion plays no role."

"As that may be, Mr Holmes, but whatever his beliefs, he'd been struck numerous times in the head with an axe—"

My jaw dropped at the news.

"—but the final blow—what do the Frenchies call it, the '*coup de grâce*'? —split open his skull. Some bloke who'd come by to do business with him at a quarter-to-eight discovered the body just inside the flat. The door had been left ajar."

"My word," I murmured.

"That's not all of it, Doctor. Recall there was a second victim. This same fellow also found a woman, presumably the pawnbroker's wife. She was lying in the doorway between the sitting room and the bedroom. Her skull was split open as well, only in her case one blow seemed sufficient to do the deed."

"My God!" I exclaimed.

"Oh, yes, Doctor. Quite shocking indeed! Blood all round. Judging from the shambles in the bedroom—drawers pulled out, chairs overturned, bed in disarray—we reckon robbery was the motive. No doubt, whoever it was that had an

29

earlier appointment with Gottfried, was looking for something. Needless to say, the poor wretches who live in the building claim not to have heard or seen anything."

Oh, the crime was horrible enough, but I must confess that my initial shock was not at its brutality. Rather, it was at the mention of the word "axe"—the murderer's weapon of choice in the novel I had just completed reading. (Whishaw translated the word as "hatchet", the same term Lomax had used in the Library to pique my interest.) And, strangely enough, in Dostoevsky's book it was a pawnbroker in the most impoverished section of St Petersburg that had also been the major victim.

Sherlock Holmes remained unimpressed. "I was anticipating a greater challenge, Lestrade," he yawned and stared into the fire. "Axe-murders and theft in the East End? You were quite right. 'Routine business,' just as you said. Certainly not stimulating enough to distract me from my scientific endeavours. I leave it to the local authorities to pursue justice for the dead." With a tone of finality, Holmes began to rise.

At the same time, a smile worked its way across the Inspector's face. "Save for this, Mr Holmes." With those intriguing words, Lestrade withdrew from his jacket pocket what at first glance looked to be a small gift. Partially wrapped in brown paper and encircled by red twine, it appeared a trifle larger than a deck of playing cards. To my great surprise, it too mirrored a clue that I recalled from Dostoevsky's novel.

At the sight of the package, Holmes' steel-grey eyes lit up. I had seen that look of keen interest present itself before— it was the same excited expression that appeared whenever a challenging puzzle seemed imminent. Sitting down again, Holmes held out his hand and gestured impatiently for Lestrade to place the package in his open palm.

With not a little anticipation, I watched as my friend withdrew a flat block of wood from the opened bloom of paper he was holding. The wood was topped with a congruent piece of lead about one-quarter inch thick. Turning the object over in his long fingers, Holmes examined it from all sides.

"Call it a loose end, Mr Holmes," said Lestrade. "We found it on the floor near Gottfried's body. It was open just as it is now. It must have been in his hands when he was struck down—though I'll be damned if I can figure out what the blasted thing is."

I was fully prepared to shed light on the matter. Dostoevsky describes a similarly wrapped package offered by the murderer to distract his victim's attention. But with Holmes' examining the paper through his magnifying lens, I knew well enough to keep silent.

Nodding as he detected the tiny drops of crimson splatter, Holmes now focused his attention on the red string, which ended in tight little curls. Owing to the complexity of the knot, it was easy to conclude that the package had originally been tied very tightly indeed.

"Common wrapping paper and common-enough twine," observed Holmes, "materials that can be purchased anywhere."

"I thought the same," said Lestrade.

But Holmes had not completed all his remarks. "Note that the string appears stretched and the knot remains intact. The string has been pulled down and away rather than cut or untied. There's nothing written on the paper—no address, not even a name—so presumably the package was not meant to be posted or delivered—rather, an object to be presented."

"Yes, yes," said Lestrade impatiently, "but what do you make of the bloody thing itself?"

Closing his eyes as if he were conjuring a picture in his mind, Holmes formed a smile and then looked at the policeman. "Use your imagination, Lestrade. Consider the package in its original state—all wrapped up and ready to be handed to the pawnbroker. Unable to discern the contents, might he not regard it as something of value? A silver or gold cigarette case, perhaps? The size and weight are both appropriate."

Lestrade rubbed his chin. "Yes, but he couldn't be certain, could he? He'd have to undo the string."

"The tightly knotted string," Holmes added.

"Says *you*, Mr Holmes." Lestrade scratched his head. "No disrespect intended, I'm sure, but in the end this thing is junk. Why would anyone tie it up like that?"

I could restrain myself no longer. "Gentlemen!" I cried out. "How better to distract the pawnbroker? Give the man something that requires time and concentration to open—then strike him down with the axe when he is preoccupied trying to unwrap it. Why, I have just read about such a crime in this book!" And I held up the thick volume I was still holding.

"A good theory, Doctor," said Lestrade stroking his chin again. "But *any* wrapped bauble would do the trick. Why add the piece of metal?"

Ignoring my reference to the book I had just waved in front of them, Holmes supplied the explanation. "By itself, the piece of wood is too light to suggest anything of value. It may be an appropriate size, but it lacks the heft. Top it with a piece of lead, however, and you have an object that, when concealed in wrapping paper, might actually seem to be something of some value—a false pledge, one might call it. And whilst the poor man was fixated on unfastening the string and paper, what could be easier—as friend Watson has already suggested—than to attack him from behind?"

Lestrade bit his upper lip as he considered the theory. "Splendid!" he said at last. "Now all we have to do is track the villain down."

"Do you mind if I take a look at the murder scene, Lestrade?" asked Holmes. "In the end, this case does seem to offer a few points of interest."

Lestrade was quick to nod his approval. Though he never liked admitting his dependence on Sherlock Holmes, the Inspector had, after all, come to my friend for advice.

Holmes turned to me. "Care to join us, Watson?"

Needless to say, I readily agreed. "I have no patients today. And the similarities to the case about which I was just reading"—for emphasis, I again brandished the book—"have attracted my interest."

"No need to carry that thing along," offered Holmes. "I am certain we shall do quite well without the aid of Mr Dostoevsky."

Lestrade responded with a look of confusion. Nonetheless, he agreed to convey the two of us to the scene of the murders. A police van waited outside; and after bundling ourselves in heavy coats and marching down the stairs, we climbed into the four-wheeler. At the crack of the driver's whip, it lurched forward and, rattling down Baker Street, proceeded to turn left into the Marylebone Road and make its way eastward across the city.

*****

It was a gloomy drive through London on a dimly-lit November morning. Dark clouds covered the sun, and a thick fog hung about us. A journey to the site of two deaths prompts little idle chatter in general, and we three sat with our private thoughts as we plunged onward. In point of fact, as I gazed out the windows of the police van, I fancied how similar were the monstrous images of desperation in the novel I had just finished reading and those depressing scenes that we were now about to face in reality.

Poverty blighted all. The East End attracted the poorest wretches from the various corners of the world—Jews from Eastern Europe most recently. Located downwind from the city and originally established beyond the city's limits, the area presented the foulest-smelling occupations imaginable. Tanneries and fulling mills poisoned the air; thick fog clogged the atmosphere; dampness from the river extended throughout the backstreets and warrens. Inconsistency reigned. Industries rose and fell; docks opened and closed; workers lost their jobs; beggars roamed the streets; prostitution, thievery, and murder thrived.

Not even the spiritual reputation of the religious could escape the shadow of the East End. The dead man and his wife had lived in a rundown boarding house in Brick Lane in Spitalfields not far from the Whitechapel Road. Though we did not know it at the time—the atrocities performed by Jack the

Ripper were still months away—the fact that such unspeakable crimes could take place in this part of the city surprised no one familiar with the area. For generations, a legacy of terror would haunt the inhabitants of the East End.

The uniformed constable standing watch at the entrance to the house in Brick Lane sprang to attention at the arrival of the police van. Following Lestrade, we made our way up the few steps to the outer door. No sooner did the Inspector push it open than we were assaulted by waves of stench—burnt oil, hot grease, overcooked chicken, singed garlic—the residue of foreign cooking, I surmised.

Lestrade made for the stairs, but Holmes paused to have a look about the entryway and the floor round the base of the staircase. In the weak light permeating the begrimed window next to the outer door, Holmes directed our attention to a small closet built into the wall beneath the stairs.

Only after holding up his glass to examine its wooden doorframe did he open the small door to reveal the confines of the tiny chamber. Clearly the domain of the caretaker, the darkened interior could not have been more than three feet square and five feet high. In it were arrayed a broom, a mop, and a bucket.

"Not much room for a hidey, I daresay," observed Lestrade.

Yet plenty of room, I could not help thinking, for any one of the miserable human beings observed by Dostoevsky who, rather than face immediate death, would willingly choose to spend the rest of their lives stranded on just such a "yard of surface" (as translated by Whishaw; "square yard" Mrs Garnett would more felicitously call it).

"There is space enough in this closet," said Holmes, "to conceal the vilest of villains." Then sinking to his knees, he scrutinised the splintered flooring just before the door. "Aha!" he exclaimed a moment later as he rubbed his fingers over the wood. "A spot of blood. Too much unsettled dust and dirt to draw more specific conclusions."

Now he held up his glass to examine more of the area surrounding the closet. I might have predicted what he would find. In the shadows a few paces to the left of the small door he stooped over and pointed to a tiny box covered in black velveteen.

"A jeweller's case," said he, picking it up.

"Blimey," muttered Lestrade. "My men missed that."

"Note the finger-marks in blood on the top," said Holmes. "No doubt they come from the murder scene." He flipped it open, and the spring-charged lid made a small popping sound as it gaped wide.

Resting inside on a bed of black velvet, lay a pair of gold drop-earrings, both about one-half inch in length and curiously shaped in a figure-eight design. "Infinity," Holmes murmured. Within each of the twin golden loops was set a small stone of polished black onyx.

"Why," Lestrade said, "the box must have been dropped by the killer on his way out. Some of his stolen loot."

"Or perhaps he was hiding in the closet," I dared venture, "to avoid people on the stairs. He might have dropped it then."

Lestrade knit his brow at my suggestion, but I was merely repeating the events from Dostoevsky's novel. There too a pair of earrings is found near the murdered pawnbroker's flat, stolen earrings inadvertently dropped by the murderer as he takes refuge behind an open door.

"These earrings do not appear to be of especially high value," Holmes observed, "but quite capable of producing a small sum as a pledge to the pawnbroker."

Holmes rose and, brushing off his trousers, handed the tiny box to the Inspector "Now, Lestrade," Holmes announced whilst the policeman was slipping the box into a side-pocket of his great coat, "to the murder scene."

I followed Holmes and Lestrade toward the dark stairwell, and slowly we made our way up the narrow steps. Gottfried and his wife had lived on the third storey. Flickering like votive lights, small candles sat on tiny shelves at the landings; and bony fingers clawed round the edges of nearby doors as the people within peered out between the narrow gaps to see the commotion on the stairs. The wide eyes we could discern might have belonged to frightened animals in the brush.

A second uniformed constable braced to attention as Lestrade marched by and pushed open the door to reveal the murder scene. Immediately, the thick cloying smell of death overwhelmed all else.

Chapter Two
The Scene of the Crime

The bodies of Gottfried and his wife lay before us, their heads split open and cradled in pools of blood.

Call me paranoiac. Or haunted. Perhaps my brain had marinated not too long but too deeply in the brine of Dostoevsky's murderous tale. Pray, forgive me, but the horrific sight framed through the doorway seemed nothing less than a twisted restaging of the gruesome abattoir in the opening section of the Russian novel.

The old man had fallen face down, his feet a few paces from the door, his hands stretched out above his head. I could barely make out the edge of a greying beard that extended some six inches below his chin. The woman lay on her back nearby, her features beribboned with blood. It seemed an almost perfect re-creation.

Lestrade began to step forward; but Holmes, desirous of examining the scene on his own, extended an arm to bar the way. Even before entering, he wanted to inspect the doorway. Ironically, Dostoevsky made much of doorways and thresholds and corridors and stairs in his book, those narrow passageways where people seem forced to encounter one another.

"Note the *mezuzah*," said Holmes, pointing to a small cylinder of reddish wood that was nailed to the inside of the doorpost. The thing had been affixed on an angle, the top leaning inward.

"Here," said Lestrade, "I've seen others like that. What do they mean?"

"Some day," said my friend, "I shall have to write a monograph on the significance of religious trinkets. There is much to be learned from the history of objects like the Catholic rosary or the Hindu *bindi*."

"Mr Holmes!" grumbled an impatient Lestrade, "can we please get on with it?"

Holmes waved away his complaint. "The *mezuzah* comes from the Hebrew for 'doorpost'. A small scroll of holy writ resides within. The observant Jew believes that placing one of these at his door signifies that God is watching over the home."

"Much good that it did," I said.

"Mumbo-jumbo," scoffed Lestrade. "Like those Golem murders in Limehouse a few years past."

Ignoring the remark, Holmes instructed us to remain in the corridor. Then he carefully entered the flat.

From the doorway, I could see that the religious atmosphere permeated the interior as well. A pair of tall, silver candlesticks stood on the mantel (too large, perhaps, for the murderer to steal); next to them, a small, carved wooden box (for spices, I would learn later); white tendrils of fringe from the dead man's prayer shawl worn under his shirt spilled out at his waist onto the blue carpeting. A round, black skullcap lay in a pool of gore not far from his head. The bloody cap had been sliced in half along the diameter, both pieces remaining oddly connected only at their ends. It was as if the sharp blade had split the cloth but spared the thread.

Holmes fell to his knees again, this time to examine the floor round the dead pawnbroker. Through his glass, he observed the wood boards and threadbare rug leading from the door to the deceased. Next he ran the lens over the old man's body. The pawnbroker was dressed in white shirt, black waistcoat, and black trousers. In particular, Holmes scrutinised the dead man's outstretched hands and fingers.

Minutes passed before he completed the grim task. Then, still holding the lens before him, he crawled on his knees the few feet between the pawnbroker's body and that of the woman—Mrs Gottfried it would later be confirmed. Her wound too was the work of the axe blade, for the top of her skull was split in halves. What was left of her fractured crown was covered with a dark kerchief similarly rent in two. Her matted hair appeared to be grey, but the exact colour was difficult to determine owing to the thick clots of blood surrounding the wound.

Holmes inspected the woman in the same fashion he had examined her husband, then stood and began surveying the room itself. He scrutinised the blood spray that mottled the walls, floor, and ceiling and viewed the tables, bookshelves, and double-globed gas lamp, which still remained lit.

Only when he moved on to the bedroom did he motion us into the flat. Even after we had entered, however, Lestrade and I continued to watch Holmes at work. As Lestrade had reported, the bedroom had been ransacked. Nonetheless,

Holmes picked his way between two fallen chairs, peered into the drawers that had been pulled out, peeked under the bed whose mattress had been awkwardly turned on its wooden frame, looked into a small metal chest that stood open on the floor near the bed, and examined the random objects on the shelves—tiny boxes, small bottles, books, and the like—most of which at had been knocked about.

Finally, he brushed himself off again and re-entered the sitting room.

"Well, Mr Holmes," asked Lestrade, "what have you learned?"

"First and foremost, Lestrade, I found that your men have marched all over the flat obfuscating most of whatever tell-tale marks the floor may have revealed."

"We had to determine that foul play had been committed. Without such a determination, I never would have come to Baker Street."

"With all this blood?" I uttered in profound disbelief. "Did you think they had taken some sort of poison?"

Lestrade ignored my sarcasm. "What else did you discover then?" he asked Holmes.

"I suggest to you that the killer is a young man who stands about five-foot-eight-inches high. He has little money, was probably a student, and though no doubt a deep thinker, maintains a two-sided nature, struggling between good and evil, the so-called *homo duplex*. At least, such a portrait is the one that our the villain would have us accept."

It was, of course, a perfect description of Raskolnikov, Dostoevsky's fictional murderer, but I let that pass.

Lestrade arched an eyebrow. "And how the deuce did you figure all that?"

"Generally speaking, this appears to be a young man's crime, performed by a person with enough agility and determination to wield an axe. Since no weapon has been found, I assume he brought it with him."

"How can you be so certain he didn't pick up such a weapon here and take it away with him?" Lestrade wanted to know.

Because Raskolnikov brought his own, I found myself thinking.

Holmes smiled. "The key to it all, Lestrade, is that package you showed us in Baker Street, the one you found on the floor by the body. As Watson has already suggested, the reason it was fastened so tightly was to command the pawnbroker's attention. The murderer knew before he ever got here how he would attack his victim. He had no choice but to bring the weapon along."

I appreciated the recognition from Holmes even though it was Dostoevsky who had laid out the original plan.

"As we have already proposed," Holmes continued, 'the pawnbroker would assume something of value was inside and concentrate all his effort on untying the complicated knot. There are red fibres from the string under his nails that suggest how hard he worked at it before finally giving up in frustration and simply forcing the string to come off. Remember too that by 7 it was quite dark so that Gottfried required light to examine the pledge. Notice how his body is directed towards the lamp on the table. What is more, one can see where the package fell when he was struck."

My gaze followed the direction in which Holmes' forefinger was pointing. In the midst of the blood spray, a small rectangular void clearly revealed where the dropped package had lain during the vicious attack.

"So intent must Gottfried have been in the process of opening it that he made a fatal mistake. Turning his back on the person who had brought it allowed the villain the opportunity to land the mortal blow. The murderer's height can be reckoned based on the placement of the strike—not atop the crown of the pawnbroker, who stood at about six feet, but slightly to the rear of the skull."

"The killer might simply have missed his aim," I offered.

"True, Watson, he might have indeed—except that the wound to the woman, who was shorter than Gottfried, is still not as high up on the skull as a taller man would have landed it. No doubt she interrupted the bloody assault upon her husband and suffered the fate of many an unlucky witness who stumbles across a crime in progress."

"And your remarks concerning his psychological nature, this two-sided business?" I asked.

"One infers he was impoverished—hence, his need for a pawnbroker and the subsequent robbery. I should expect he was a regular customer of Samuel Gottfried, for why else would Gottfried have dared to turn his back? On the one hand, the killer planned at some length to commit the crime. And yet in his haste to search for loot to plunder, he overlooked a drawer at the bottom of the bureau containing a number of five-pound notes. He did locate a chest beneath the bed and managed to open it, but for whatever the reason he did not feel he could spend the time looking for more. A meticulous planner, but a distracted executioner."

I nodded. Raskolnikov too had stolen from a chest hidden under a bed, and he also had overlooked money kept elsewhere that would have been his for the taking. "But a deep thinker, Holmes, a student? Certainly that is quite a leap."

"You'll note that atop the bookshelf in the sitting room lies a volume of lectures by Thomas Carlyle titled *On Heroes, Hero-Worship, and the Heroic in History.* There are fresh blood smears on the cover and on the edges of the pages, but no spray. There can be little doubt that the murderer handled the book, but not until after committing the crime. One must conclude, therefore, that it was placed atop the shelf after the Gottfrieds had been dispatched by someone familiar with the text."

"Surely, Holmes," I protested, "you're not suggesting that the killer took the time to seek out a book by Thomas Carlyle in the library of Samuel Gottfried?"

"On the contrary, Watson. "Though a religious man might have any number of philosophical works on his shelf, I believe that in this case the book was purposely left in that prominent spot by the murderer. Curious, is it not? Insufficient time to rob the place, but opportunity enough to set out a copy of Carlyle's lectures in a place where we could find it. Oh, I think we must credit our villain with intellectual tastes that go beyond the common workingman."

"I'm afraid I don't follow," said Lestrade.

I did. Carlyle's collected lectures promoted theories about the so-called great men of history. Even a cursory reading of *Crime and Punishment* would reveal Raskolnikov's admiration for Napoleon, a figure whom Carlyle addresses in his final lecture. Thanks to Dostoevsky, the entire crime seemed straightforward to me.

"If you say so, Mr Holmes," said Lestrade, shaking his head. "In any case, we shall keep our eyes peeled for just such a man."

"And request that patrons of Mr Gottfried report to the police the outstanding pledges they have left with him. A few trinkets remain in the drawers; what is reported missing may enable you to ensnare the villain if he should be among those who show up to claim them."

"Thank you very much indeed, Mr Holmes," said Lestrade. "I pride myself on recognizing the help you sometimes have to offer. I shall deposit you and Dr Watson back in Baker Street and then return to the Yard to file my report."

Following the Inspector's lead, we retraced our steps down the dark stairwell. With the doors nearest the landings still cracked open as we marched past, we could sense the flat-dwellers behind them who could not refrain from peeping out again to see why the police were lingering in their building.

An explosion of light hit us upon exiting the premises. There had been so much gloom inside that one could be excused for having forgotten that it was yet the middle of the day.

Chapter Three

Comparisons

Attentive readers will recall that in *A Study in Scarlet*, I labelled as "nil" Sherlock Holmes' knowledge of literature. Oh, Holmes could be counted on for the odd factoid regarding important authors and their works—witness his knowledge of Carlyle at the scene of the Gottfried murders—but I would not classify him a student of *belles lettres*. For that matter, neither could I apply such a label to myself—at least, not yet. Of the two lodgers at 221B, however, I felt that with my first narrative to be published in less than a fortnight, I could lay greater claim to such a title than he.

In the van carrying us back to Baker Street, therefore, I assumed it was I alone who was pondering the parallels between an active murder investigation and the horrors of the fictional work to which my friend at the library had introduced me. A dead pawnbroker and flat-mate, a murderous axe, a hurried robbery, a dropped clue, a possible student-perpetrator—even though I maintained some vague doubts, the similarities of the crimes, both fictional and real, compelled me to inform Sherlock Holmes of my conclusions.

But did I dare? I could already fancy him describing such comparisons as the naïve ruminations of a literary traveller who had somehow got blown off course. Did I want to invite even more ridicule? Might my current supposition undermine Holmes' faith in my insights? Such questions plagued me throughout our drive to Baker Street.

When we returned to our rooms, Lestrade agreed to join us for a late luncheon of roast beef sandwiches supplied by Mrs Hudson. And yet no sooner did Billy place the food before us than it became readily apparent to me that my worries were interfering with my appetite. Quite simply, I had to make public my thoughts concerning the role Dostoevsky's novel played in the macabre drama to which Lestrade had introduced us.

"*Crime and Punishment*, you say?" The Inspector raised his eyebrows and lowered his sandwich. "Good title. Describes my work. But never heard of the book, I'm afraid." What the policeman lacked in literary knowledge, however, I am pleased to say that he made up for in pertinacity. "Your conclusions may be all wrong, Doctor. This whole business might be mere coincidence. And yet the similarities you bring up do seem to raise some interesting questions."

Holmes' reaction was more pointed. Shaking his head, he said, "Dostoevsky again? Really, Watson, do you think me ignorant?" He asked this last question with an amused look and biting tone. "You may take pleasure in underestimating my familiarity with literary art; but do not forget that, like you, I too have read the galleys of your account of the Lauriston Gardens murder, and so I know that you yourself employed the word 'immense' to describe my knowledge of sensational literature."

He was correct about that.

"*You* might place *Crime and Punishment* on a lofty plane, old fellow, but I would relegate it to a more common category. Why, in a letter to his publisher, Dostoevsky himself called the book a "psychological account of a crime." No, I believe 'sensational literature' is quite the accurate label."

Holmes' voice was spirited, but his features remained without expression. Not only did I feel corrected, but insulted as well.

Nor was he finished. "Do you think that I had not already recognised the comparisons you bring up, Watson? Do you regard me as so obtuse? After all, I do my best to keep informed on writings—fictional or otherwise—related to the criminal world.

"But if antecedents for these horrific crimes need be mentioned at all, let me assure you that Dostoevsky's novel, which you deem so relevant, remains a less fruitful object of study than two real crimes that occurred the year before he completed the book. It was these criminal acts that doubtlessly formed the basis for his fictitious killings."

I shook my head in silent confession to being unaware of either event.

"I refer, of course, to the 1865 murders of two old women in Moscow and another in St Petersburg. And I do not even speak of the villainous Karakozov, the sickly, failed student who attempted to assassinate the Tsar in '66 at the very time Dostoevsky was in the midst of writing the early part of the novel—an event, I might add, that for any number of reasons, interfered with his usual production of prose. You will recall that *Crime and Punishment* first appeared in serial instalments."

I suppose I should have expected such a riposte. It was just the sort that Holmes often aimed my way following one of my ill-considered attempts to promote my knowledge. It was not unlike our discussion in the sketch I titled "A Case of Identity" involving the jilted Miss Mary Sutherland. In that exchange, Holmes vowed to keep piling fact upon fact until I acknowledged him to be right. "You see, but do not observe," he was fond of saying to me.

As for the Russian crimes to which Holmes had referred, I could offer only the feeblest of retorts: "But, sadly, Holmes, murders occur so frequently. How can you be certain that the particular killings you singled out actually inspired Dostoevsky?"

Holmes emitted a dry chuckle. "Why, the parallels are obvious, Watson. In the Moscow case, the murder weapon was an axe. And as in Brick Lane, the scene of the crimes had been ransacked and the victims robbed of gold jewellery, jewellery—I might add—which had been hidden by their employer, like Dostoevsky's pawnbroker, in an iron chest. What is more, my dear Watson, the killer, one Gerasim Chistov, was said to be a member of the religious denomination called 'Old Believers'. Do you know the Russian word for the member of such a group?"

Needless to say, I did not—though I was beyond certain that Holmes did.

"*Raskolnik*, old fellow. It comes from the Russian *raskol* for 'dissenter', one who separates himself from a traditional point of view—or, at the risk of invoking the imagery of the axe—one who *splits*."

I felt truly defeated. Clearly, Holmes knew that the name of Dostoevsky's murderer was 'Raskolnikov'."[6]

In spite of a yawn offered up by Lestrade, Holmes continued to defend his account of the criminal behaviours that might have influenced Dostoevsky. "In the other example, I mentioned," said he, "a Mrs Dubarasova was murdered in St Petersburg just as Dostoevsky was beginning to write his

---

[6] The transliteration of Russian into English is a tricky business. Whilst the spellings of Fred Whishaw constituted my initial encounter with the rendering of Russian names, I have chosen to employ the spellings of Constance Garnett in this account since hers have become much more recognizable to the English-reading public. Thus, "Raskolnikov" for "Raskolnikoff", "Porfiry" for "Porphyrius", "Ilya" for "Elia", etc. (JHW)

novel. What is key in the Dubarasova case, Watson—as I am sure you will not fail to note—is that the poor woman had been distracted by a false package presented to her by the killer. All the St Petersburg newspapers reported the story, and Dostoevsky was certain to have read of it."

Lestrade mulled over the details. "The St Petersburg newspapers, you say. A false package?"

Holmes nodded. "For that matter," said he, "I have yet to mention the traditional association, the case that most criminal experts argue shaped Dostoevsky's thinking. How else to account for the references he recorded in his published preface to the transcripts of the trial concerning the French murderer Lacenaire?"

Lacenaire—another name I had never heard before.

"Although the Frenchman's crimes took place some fifty years ago," Holmes explained, "not only was he responsible for at least two deaths, one with an axe, but he also shared many similarities with Dostoevsky's killer. Both were educated; both were poor. Both had anti-social beliefs, about which they wrote in public journals. Lacenaire challenged the penal system; Raskolnikov, you may recall, defended the very nature of crime itself in an article he wrote. As a result of their ruminations, both came to view murder as protest and hoped for the ascendancy of a superman—what the Germans call the *Übermensch*—to set society right. Why, Dostoevsky himself called the case more compelling than anything he had found in fiction."

We continued eating in silence though throughout the remainder of our meal Holmes maintained a triumphant smile that seemed altogether unworthy of someone considered a friend.

Lestrade, on the other hand, seemed to be pondering my observations. Minutes passed before he spoke again. Then he asked, "Roosians, you say, Doctor?"

I nodded.

"I may have a few connections in that area," said he, taking a final bite of his sandwich. "Just lately, many of them Russkies—anarchists and Nihilists they call themselves—have come to England to create trouble with their radical ideas. To get themselves out of tight fixes—or more than likely, to earn a few quid—a goodly number have turned informer. Now that we suspect there might be a Roosian flavour to these murders, I think I'll just nose round a bit and see if any of them have something to say about what went on in Brick Lane." On that note of possibility, Lestrade employed his napkin to wipe clean his mouth.

"Must get back to the Yard," said he, rising from the table. "We have a murderer to catch."

Chapter Four
Another Case

At the door, Inspector Lestrade barely managed to avoid colliding with Billy the page.

The boy had arrived to announce a client. "Miss Priscilla Cheek," he proclaimed.

As Lestrade made his way towards the stairs, he none too discreetly took the time to admire the lady from stately crown to dainty toe. Doubtlessly inured to such rude glances, the handsome young woman, draped in a long, black woollen coat and wearing a small, round purple hat, walked determinedly into our sitting room.

I took her coat whilst Holmes pointed Billy to the luncheon dishes left standing and, with the wave of a hand, indicated their removal. Ignoring the clatter of the table business, Holmes ushered our visitor to the chair facing the window. He sat opposite, as was his wont in hearing new cases, allowing whatever was left of the dwindling daylight behind him to hide his own facial reactions in the contrasting darkness of his silhouette.

"Miss Cheek," said Holmes, "may I introduce to you my friend and colleague, Dr John Watson. Whatever you wish to say to me may be spoken in front of him as well."

"Charmed," said I, hoping my compliment had not been obliterated by the rattle of dishes as Billy vacated the premises.

Miss Cheek managed a brief smile, but then immediately turned to address my friend. In her frock of purple velvet, she presented quite the picture of a determined young lady. "It is about my brother Roderick that I have come to see you, Mr Holmes." So saying, she removed from her reticule a photograph of a handsome young man in the black vestments and white collar of a school uniform and handed the picture to my friend. "Please keep it. It may help you in the matter I've come to discuss."

"Why, he could be your twin," observed Holmes. "Despite the difference in gender, your appearances seem quite similar."

"We are indeed twins," she replied with a shy smile.

I leaned in Holmes' direction to view the photograph he was holding. The young man had the same firm jawline and expressive dark eyes as his sister. "You make quite the handsome pair," said I.

This time Miss Cheek blushed crimson. "Thank you, Doctor; but pleasantries aside, my brother has gone missing, and I am quite concerned." To my friend, she said, "I would like you to find him, Mr Holmes. I am twenty-one and due to be married shortly. Our mother and father are dead, you see, and we have only ourselves to look after each other. Worrying about poor Roderick is the last thing I want on my mind."

Sherlock Holmes propped the photograph against a stack of books on a nearby table and, steepling his long fingers beneath his chin, leaned back in his chair.

"I live in a boarding house for women in Norwood," Miss Cheek continued. "Roderick and I were both of age when our parents died in a terrible carriage accident. They left us a bit of money, most of which, Roderick and I agreed, was to be used for his schooling. Before he went missing, you see, he had hoped to become a barrister; and he was reading for the law at King's College here in London. He couldn't afford rooms in the Inns of Court, but he did find a small flat not far from Somerset House."

"Quite ambitious," said I.

"Indeed, Doctor," replied Miss Cheek. "I thought my brother to be the most ambitious of students until I got a letter from him informing me that, due to a lack of funds, he had given up his studies. I possessed some money of my own, and I immediately went round to his rooms just off Kingsway to give it to him."

"Did you find him there?" I asked.

She smiled wistfully. "No, he had already gone, and his landlord knew nothing of his whereabouts. I imagine it was just as well. If he had known where Roderick had got off to, I should think he would have tracked him down to collect the rent still owed. As it was, thanks to the money intended for my brother, I was able to settle the matter with the landlord myself."

"Most responsible of you," said I. One need not be versed in the field of psychology to recognise that bonds between siblings can be amongst the strongest in the world, especially regarding twins.

Blushing once more, Miss Cheek continued her narrative. "Most fortunately, a pleasant young man who had lodgings in that very building overheard my conversation regarding Roderick. Accompanying me to the street, he said that although he would never tell the landlord, he knew that Roderick had moved to new lodgings and had been tutoring young children to help pay his school costs and lower rent. But as one might expect, Roderick's earnings didn't amount to much; and once he ran out of money, he decided to forgo his schooling and look elsewhere for an even cheaper place to live."

"Did this young man have any idea where that 'elsewhere' might be?" Holmes asked.

"All he would say was that Roderick had found a room in the East End—where rents aren't so dear."

" . . . And life is miserable," I felt compelled to add.

"Which is precisely the reason," added Miss Cheek in reaction to my harsh assessment, "that this otherwise kindly fellow refused to give me the exact address. He said that Roderick told him that if I ever came to ask, the gentleman should not to worry his sister." She shook her head in frustration. "Oh, gentlemen, we are not rich people, but neither are we so impoverished that Roderick should have to take lodgings in so desperate a part of the city."

"Obviously," said I, "your brother has made no effort to contact you."

"I think Roderick is too ashamed, Doctor. I know I would be if I were in similar straits."

"However unhappy it may make you," Holmes said, "if one has reached one's majority—as you said you both have done—there is no crime in withholding from family members the location of one's residence."

At this juncture, I risk authorial intrusion to remind my readers that Holmes and I entertained any number of different investigations simultaneously. Contrary to the idea perpetuated by the many individual cases I have chronicled, significant numbers began well before others ended; and though we were simultaneously involved in the investigation of the double murders in Brick Lane, there was no reason to suspect any sort of connection between those deaths and the disappearance of this woman's brother.

Nonetheless, with Dostoevsky's novel fresh in my mind, various events in Miss Cheek's account jumped out at me. For instance, before committing his horrific murders,

Raskolnikov, like Roderick Cheek, had been studying for the law, had tutored children, and had moved to dingy lodgings in an impoverished area. Though not a twin, Raskolnikov too had a handsome sister, one Dounia by name. And like the attractive young woman seated before us, Dounia was also planning to marry.

Dostoevsky and his novel bedevil me! I suddenly screamed inside my head. Was I going mad? One glance at the charming Miss Cheek should have rendered me incapable of thinking her twin responsible for any sort of foul act, let alone the ghastly axe murders committed by Raskolnikov.

Still, I had to ask. "Miss Cheek, do you know if your brother ever frequented a pawn broker?"

Holmes sprang to his feet. "Really, Watson, let us not go in that direction! Let me assure you, Miss Cheek, that I have associates well placed in the East End who should soon be able to locate your brother. They know the area, and they are especially alert to newcomers."

In spite of the abruptness of Holmes' interruption, I retained enough composure to appreciate that Miss Cheek had not answered my question. Holmes had mentioned associates in the East End. To whom was he referring? I wondered.

Before I could ask any further questions, however, he escorted our visitor to the door; assured her that his fees would be acceptable to her budget; and before conducting her to the stairs, recorded her address in Norwood so he could notify her when there was news.

No sooner had he closed the door than Sherlock Holmes turned and admonished me once more. "Watson, I insist that you not bring up that Dostoevsky humbug in every case we encounter. Had you never read the book, you would not be making such connections. What is next? Will you read Miss Bronte's *Jane Eyre* and begin searching for mad women in every attic you espy?"

Yet another rebuke, and his previous complaint still ringing in my ears. His criticisms always stung—especially when delivered with that wry smile he was just then displaying. "Now," said he "I shall meet with the Baker Street Irregulars."

The group to whom Holmes referred consisted of his personal collection of street urchins. In their ragged and dirty clothes, they could travel the byways of London and raise no suspicions, especially in the squalor of the East End from where a number of them hailed.

Dostoevsky may have rightly bemoaned the ill treatment of St Petersburg's "gutter children" (to employ Mrs Garnett's translation), but at least here in London Holmes offered such youths practical employment. He paid the lads handsomely for their services though I thought that calling them "associates" seemed to be gilding the lily, as it were.

"With this likeness of the missing person," Holmes said, picking up the photograph of Roderick Cheek, "I have little doubt they shall find him post-haste."

*****

When I came down for breakfast the next morning, Sherlock Holmes, attired in ear-flapped travelling cap, wool scarf, and Inverness cape, appeared ready for cold weather. More to the point, he was carrying his Gladstone.

"I have a trip to make, Watson. It shall take me out of the country for a number of days—perhaps a week or more. I shall give you a full report upon my return."

"Where—?" I began to ask, but he was already out the door. Holmes would frequently go off somewhere on his own and leave me in the dark. Yet seldom did he do so at the start of a new case—or two new cases, to be precise. With nothing left to do just then, I turned my attention to the breakfast of kippers and eggs that Mrs Hudson had left waiting for me on the table. There was no sense in letting the food go to waste.

Chapter Five

Voices from the East End

Not two hours after Holmes' abrupt departure, Charlie Duffle, the leader of the Irregulars, came to present his findings.

"We found the bloke Mr 'Olmes was looking for, Dr Watson." he announced proudly. "No trouble at all." Returning the picture Holmes had lent him, he pointed to the face of Roderick Cheek. "'E's hid out in a place in Goulston Street, hain't 'e?"

Having spied the person in the photograph walking along a side street, one of the young watchers conveyed this information up the chain of command. Thus, it was Charlie himself who took up the hunt; waited for Roderick Cheek to reappear; and when he did, followed him to a boarding house in Goulston Street.

"Fourth floor," Charlie added with a proud grin and furnished me the address along with the room's number. In point of fact, the building was not far from Brick Lane, the scene of the pawnbroker's murder. Promising to share with his mates the agreed-upon sum established by Holmes, the lad took his payment and bolted down the stairs.

No sooner had he exited than I faced a decision. Should I wait for Holmes' return to question Roderick Cheek, or should I take it upon myself to perform the interrogation? Actually, my choice seemed obvious. Not only was there no way of knowing for how long Holmes would be gone, but there also remained the possibility that if Cheek changed his lodgings, we could lose sight of the elusive fellow once again.

I must also confess that another thought continued to intrigue me. With Holmes away, I might more freely pursue the line of thought, which I simply could not get out of my head—the uncanny relationship between Cheek's behaviour and that of Dostoevsky's fictional protagonist.

Ultimately, it was justice for the two bloodied corpses I had viewed the day before that prompted me into action. I slipped Cheek's photograph into my jacket pocket, put on my heavy overcoat, marched down the stairs, and proceeded out to the kerb.

*****

"Goulston Street," the hansom driver repeated. "Sure you want t' go there, Guv?"

Assuring him that I was, I climbed in and almost immediately fell back against the red-leather cushion as the hansom shot off down Baker Street and not long thereafter turned east into Oxford Street. The more eastward we travelled, the more the scenery devolved from the stately Georgian architecture and ordered parks and squares of Bloomsbury to the run-down warehouses and dingy living quarters of the East End. The cab finally came to a halt before an uninviting rooming house of five storeys.

The cab took off as soon as I paid the driver, no one wanting to remain longer than necessary in that section of the city. For my part, I turned my attention to the dark-brick building before me, the reported dwelling place of Roderick Cheek. On the ground floor stood a small shop selling Jewish foods. I could make out the name "Lindermann" on a faded

75

sign, the block Roman letters contrasting with the curls and flourishes of the seriffed Hebrew script that anointed much of the front wall and windows.

A few paces to the left of the shop, a weathered black door led into the gloomy foyer of the boarding house itself. Immediately upon entering, I was struck by the same rancid smells that had assaulted my senses in the building in Brick Lane.

Slowly, I climbed the darkened stairway to the fourth storey. Accompanied by the muffled shouts and cries of various inhabitants, I located the door, which Charlie Duffle had identified as belonging to Roderick Cheek, and knocked smartly upon it.

Though no sounds came from within, the door creaked open at my touch. Thick grime clung to the window glass; but with no curtains to block the light, a few feeble rays did work their way into the room. I could not help musing that the small area they illuminated resembled the claustrophobic confines of Raskolnikov's tiny flat. Dostoevsky had described the latter as "coffin-like". Confining rooms cramp the spirit, he maintained.

Though I remained standing at the portal, I could readily see that the contents were equally Spartan: a wooden table and chairs to the left, a small bed against the back wall, a chest of drawers and a small rickety shelf full of books to the right. Mildewed strips of what once might have been yellow wallpaper curled down at varying lengths from just below the crown moulding at the ceiling.

Upon the bed were heaped piles of old clothes and blankets, and it took a few moments for me to discern some movement beneath them.

"Will—William, is that you, mate?" came a muffled voice at last.

"No," I said, entering slowly, "I am afraid I am not William. I am, in fact, John Watson, a medical doctor."

A drawn, pale face burrowed up from under the blankets. Thanks to the photograph I had brought along, I concluded that in spite of a week's worth of beard, dark lines in the forehead, tangled hair, and deep shadows beneath glazed eyes, the face did indeed belong to Mr Roderick Cheek.

"Has—has William sent you? He knows I'm not well."

I took a step towards the bed in the same manner I would approach a patient. "What is wrong with you?" I asked.

"I'm burning up, Doctor. I—I have some sort of fever."

I stood next to the bed now and, applying the back of my hand to Roderick Cheek's perspiring brow, was immediately convinced that he had accurately diagnosed his condition. A metal cup and glass water-pitcher had been placed on a chair next to the bed. I filled the cup with water and placed it in his shaking hand. He raised the cup to his lips and slowly drank.

I waited for him to put down the cup, and then I spoke of my true intentions. "I'm afraid, Mr Cheek, that you have welcomed me under false pretences. I have not come here to examine your health."

The ailing young man struggled to sit up. With his feverish eyes, he examined me closely. "Then what—what are you doing here?" he demanded.

The very question I was asking myself. What could I hope to determine by questioning someone in so sickly a condition? "I am the associate of Mr Sherlock Holmes, the consulting detective. Perhaps you are familiar with his name."

Exhaling and falling back against a limp pillow, Cheek shook his head. "Never heard of him. What's this got to do with me?"

"Your sister came—"

"Priscilla sent you?"

"Your sister is deeply concerned about your welfare, Mr Cheek. She asked Sherlock Holmes to find out where you were living. She wishes to help you."

"I'm done with her!" Cheek fairly shouted. "For my sake, she insists on marrying a fool of a banker. She wants his money to enable me to succeed. I shall not allow it!" He screamed and shuddered at the same time.

Whatever his strategy—if strategy it even was—his histrionics needed to be reined in. The issue that kept gnawing at me would be the very thing to sharpen his focus. "Do you know a pawnbroker called Gottfried?" I dared to ask.

"*Samuel* Gottfried?"

Obviously, he did know the man.

Roderick Cheek paused to collect his thoughts. "I-I know him. He lives nearby. In Brick Lane. I've pawned a few items with him. I—I think he still has the watch my father gave me. Why do you ask?"

"Monday night." said I calmly, "Mr Gottfried was murdered."

Cheek's expression remained quizzical though perspiration covered his brow. He said nothing for a few moments, as if trying to come to grips with what I had told him. "And why," he asked at last, "have you come here to report this to me?"

"You were a client of the man," I said. "*Associates* for Sherlock Holmes—" (my friend's euphemism for "children" seemed reassuringly official) "—reported to me where you live, and I am here to investigate."

"Investigate? Investigate *what*? This is the first I've heard of any such murder."

"And Monday night? Where were you?"

Cheek sighed. "Like any night lately—here in bed. Look at me. I'm not well, I tell you."

I looked, but my mind was already racing ahead to the key question. If I was not the one to ask it, who would? "Tell me, Mr Cheek, have you ever read the Russian novel, *Crime and Punishment*?"

"*Crime and Punishment*? Dostoevsky?" He pulled up the dark-blue blanket to mop his forehead. "Why, yes," he said. "In school. A year ago. For a tutorial in Russian literature. But why—" here a smile broke through the man's illness—"oh, I see. In the novel, Raskolnikov murders his pawnbroker, and you're wondering if . . . . Hold on— Raskolnikov murdered the pawnbroker's sister as well. Who else besides Gottfried was killed?"

"His wife," I said. Holmes would have noted that it was Cheek himself who suggested a second victim. Cheek's next admission seemed even more incriminating.

"With an axe, no doubt." He followed this observation with a high-pitched laugh.

The synchronicity was unnerving. Though Cheek had offered no more information than the novel itself provides, Dostoevsky's killer spends much of the time after the murders in bed with a fever. Whatever else Cheek had to say, I could readily see that my visit to this foul den would do nothing to ease my suspicions.

At that moment the door swung open to reveal another young man. He was holding a large, brown earthenware pot by its handles. The grey-brown hue of his suit matched the colour of the pot.

"William," Roderick gasped. "Thank God, you've come back."

"Who's this then?" William demanded, nodding at me.

I proceeded to explain my presence as best I could. "Who are *you*?" I asked in turn.

It was the sick man who answered. "Doctor Watson, this is William Arbuthnot. We read for the law together when I was still at King's College." Another trill of laughter. "Save your breath. No need to ask. He's read Dostoevsky's novel too. We shared the same tutor, in fact, and discussed the book quite often."

"What does he want here?" asked William. "And what book is it that I am supposed to have read?"

Cheek's eyes burned with excitement. "Someone's murdered Gottfried the pawnbroker. With an axe. This crazy fellow believes that anyone who has read *Crime and Punishment* is a suspect." He turned to me. "Did I get that right? William is a suspect as well, is he not? I should judge that you wish to question him too." Again he broke into that weird laughter.

In the novel, Raskolnikov has a friend called Razumihin, who after many twists and turns ends up marrying

Raskolnikov's sister. Though I had no reason to believe William Arbuthnot to be the *fiancé* of whom Miss Cheek had spoken, he clearly filled the role of friend for her brother. And since at the very least, this William had also read the novel, I put the question to him as well, "May I ask, Mr Arbuthnot, where *you* were Monday night?"

The man answered me with a change of subject. "Let me guess," he replied, "you're one of those Christians who believe everyone suffers Original Sin."

I failed to see the logic. Besides, religion has never been a major influence in my life, and I was rather taken aback at so personal a query.

"Original Sin is a vague concept," pontificated Arbuthnot, sounding every bit like the erudite student he still was. "As a result, one school of thought believes there are sinners among us who feel they must commit a truly immoral act to give tangible reality to their guilt. Is that what you are suggesting, sir—that someone murdered the pawnbroker in order to provide himself a real crime about which to feel guilty? Is that your hypothesis?"

Suddenly, Cheek sat up and shook both his fists in the air. "Well argued, William!" he shouted.

Though an upstanding member in the Church of England, I readily acknowledge that juggling the concepts of sin and guilt is well beyond my depth. As for interpreting the theological implications of *Crime and Punishment*—well, allow me to say that I was perfectly content with Raskolnikov's repentance at the novel's conclusion. His confession sufficed. I saw no need for additional questions about why he had committed the murders.

William's intellectual response, however, suggested those new psychological interpretations that serve to undermine any sense of contrition, religious or otherwise. Indeed, I wondered if William Arbuthnot might be offering a look into his own state of mind. Whatever his thinking, I recognised that at the very least he had dodged my question concerning his whereabouts on the night of Gottfried's murder.

Whilst I pondered the meaning of all this chatter, William was placing on the chair next to the bed the pot he had been holding all the while. "Calm down, mate," he said to Cheek. "I've brought you the perfect medicine—chicken soup." Retrieving a large wooden spoon that had been lying on the table, he reported, "It's from the shop downstairs. Mrs Lindermann gave it to me when I said you were ill. 'Eat,' she told me to tell you. 'Then go to sleep. You'll be fine in the morning.'"

Roderick Cheek ignored the spoon and, taking hold of the two handles, drank directly from the pot. Some of the steaming broth trickled down his bristled chin and onto the blanket.

More concerned with the soup than with their visitor, Cheek and Arbuthnot succeeded in convincing me that it was time to leave. Though Miss Cheek's brother had indeed been located, I seemed to have uncovered a more pressing issue. Both young men were readers of *Crime and Punishment*, and either one—or both—might have appropriated the deadly plan that Dostoevsky had established in the book's opening section. Having travelled to the East End with a single suspect in mind for the Brick Lane murders, I found myself returning to Baker Street with the number doubled.

*****

Not long after I had returned to our sitting room, Inspector Lestrade arrived with a short, grizzled man in tow. Maintaining a firm hand on the man's shoulder, Lestrade marched him in as he might treat a criminal. The stranger, dressed in baggy work clothes and flat tweed cap, sported a dramatic, grey moustache that extended outward and ended in sharp, waxed points. Lestrade had previously spoken of his contacts within London's Russian community; and here, as I was about to discover, stood a living representative.

"Says his name is Dmitry," Lestrade told me as he let go of the man, "but he calls himself the Assistant, he does. Lives in the East End. Claims that before coming to England, he'd been an Assistant Superintendent with the St Petersburg police. As I recall, it's the same city where those murders in that book took place."

St Petersburg. It haunts this investigation.

"I brought him here so you could have a look, Doctor. Never can tell what valuable memories he might be storing away."

In spite of the man's drab coat and trousers, he held his shoulders back and, though not very tall, evoked the erect, formal posture of a military officer. I seemed to remember an assistant superintendent mulling about in *Crime and Punishment*, but the pleasure I was experiencing from the credence Lestrade had bestowed upon my suspicions pushed that memory out of mind.

"Actually," said Lestrade, "the Assistant here is a difficult fellow to lay hands on. He's a walking contradiction, he is. A former policeman in Petersburg who now wants nothing to do with the police—nothing, that is, except when we pay him for his information."

The man continued to stand at attention.

"I must say," Lestrade rattled on, "that he's actually provided some helpful tips about criminal goings-on among our London Russkies."

The man removed his hat. "Iss enough I tell you what you want," said he to Lestrade with a snarl. He spoke competent English with a thick Russian accent. "More I not wish to do."

"How much does he know about the murders in Brick Lane?" I asked. "Has he even heard about the pawnbroker?"

At the word "pawnbroker", the Assistant looked at me.

"Here, then," said Lestrade, catching the movement as well. "Do you know something about the death of the pawnbroker, Samuel Gottfried?"

"Gottfried?" repeated the Russian. "I give him pledge from time to time. Not lately."

"Didn't happen to see him Monday night then?" Lestrade asked.

"Not for months have I seen him. I know nothing about murder."

"So you say," Lestrade replied slowly, his manner of dragging out the words suggestive of his scepticism.

Sensing a connection to Dostoevsky, I was more direct. "What about the story of the murdered pawnbroker and her sister in St Petersburg twenty years ago?" I asked. "Two women killed with an axe and robbed."

The Assistant shrugged his shoulders. "Iss long time. I forget old cases."

Perhaps he had indeed forgotten an old case. At the same time, I wondered that he had not refuted the axe-murders as fiction.

"I work hard as policeman in Russia. On my hat, I wear—how do say? —cockade of officer; and still they sack me. Too angry, they tell me. Where is justice?"

"But do you not see a similarity between a murdered pawnbroker in St Petersburg and the murdered pawnbroker in this current case?" I was nothing if not persistent.

He shrugged once more. "Coincidence."

Coincidence—the Assistant's use of the word was itself a coincidence. For when Raskolnikov is still in the planning stages of his crime, he overhears someone talking about the benefits of killing the very same pawnbroker Raskolnikov has made his target.

To be sure, hearing that conversation truly is coincidental; but believing the words to be some sort of sign, Raskolnikov convinces himself that he should actually go ahead and commit the awful deed. After all, had Providence not been on his side, had the Fates not been interested, he obviously would have encountered no such reinforcement of his plan. In his own twisted way, Raskolnikov trusts that he is carrying out some greater design.

"Come round Scotland Yard in a day or two," Lestrade said to the Assistant. "Once we go through all the pledges that the pawnbroker held at the time of his death—that is, the ones that were not stolen—we'll be returning the items to those who come to claim them. Put the word out to everyone you know who used his services."

"I already tell you," the Assistant replied, "no pledges to Gottfried now." Then, "Can I go?"

"Yes, indeed," said Lestrade, and without another word, the Russian left—"escaped" might be a better term—and fairly bounded down the stairs. The outer door slammed shut with a resounding bang.

"I'll be taking my leave as well," said Lestrade. Before exiting, however, he turned to ask, "Any word from Holmes?"

I answered in the negative, and then it was Lestrade's turn to lumber down the stairs. Only this time, the outer door closed without a sound.

Chapter Six
Dust to Dust

On the same Wednesday evening that Lestrade and I were quizzing the Russian informer, no less a personage than Rabbi Nathan Adler, the venerable Chief Rabbi of the Great Synagogue at Duke's Place, requested the bodies of Mr and Mrs Gottfried from Scotland Yard for burial the next day.

"The Superintendent agreed straight away," Lestrade informed me with a derisive laugh. "I mean, we knew what killed them, didn't we? No need to waste time examining the corpses."

The bodies were released late Wednesday night and prepared for burial the following morning. It was Lestrade's idea to attend the service, and he invited me to come along. "You never know who might show up," said he, suddenly sounding very much the expert detective. "You never know who might take extraordinary interest in the murders. Some killers like to view the results of their handiwork."

Thursday broke dark and wet, a penetrating rain drumming on the roof of the police van, which Lestrade had commandeered to retrieve me at Baker Street. Within minutes we were circling the east side of Regent's Park and then continuing north by way of Seven Sisters Road to the Edmonton Cemetery some eight miles from the East End murder scene.

An hour later we were trundling through the cemetery's open gates marked on both sides by a pair of red-brick columns, each surmounted with a large Star of David. The cemetery had opened only a few years before, and swards of green lawn still remained unmarked by the countless gravestones inevitably destined to fill the landscape.

A protective white canopy had been set up for the Gottfrieds' funeral though what had softened to a thin rain eased to a gentle mist before the service began and ceased completely minutes later. Standing on the wet grass within in a copse of beech trees, Lestrade and I kept ourselves out-of-sight. We were close enough to distinguish words like "kind" and "caring" in the eulogy and the plaintive melodies of the prayers the rabbi was offering up. The prayers were in Hebrew, of course, and beyond our understanding; and yet the lugubrious chants conveyed the shared sadness of the people pressing close to the two open graves.

In addition to the rents in their black clothes, the adults who stood shedding tears near the rabbi—the Gottfrieds' two sons and their wives, I would learn later—all wore head coverings: the men, tall hats; the women, round affairs shielded with black lace. Also dressed in black, two young grandchildren, a boy and a girl, leaned quietly against their parents. The police, Lestrade explained, had already spoken to the family members concerning their suspicions and gained no useful information.

I might add that due to his height and slender physique, the taller of the sons put me in mind of the still absent Holmes. In fact, a single look at the man's frock coat, dangling side locks, and full beard suggested how easily one might disguise oneself. Had the young boy not suddenly grasped his father's leg, I could even imagine the tall son being the absent Holmes himself.

Others besides the family were also in attendance. Four young men were hovering a number of yards beyond the canopy. Three wore flat caps and one a bowler, their distance from the graves as well as their conventional attire suggesting little connection to either the family or to the religion.

On closer inspection I realized I recognized two of them. The unshaven one in a short jacket and flat hat turned out to be Roderick Cheek; his friend William Arbuthnot, better equipped for the rain in a long mac and bowler, stood by his side. At a respectful distance from the burial site two gravediggers leaned upon the wooden handles of their upright shovels.

"If I had to guess," offered Lestrade, "I would say that group of four were clients of the pawnbroker."

"I should imagine so," I responded, without revealing what I already knew about two of them.

After the caskets had been lowered into the ground, the mourners formed a short queue by the two graves and one by one wielded the gravediggers' shovels to deposit soil atop the lids. The children filled their fists with dirt and tossed their handfuls into each grave. The moist dirt splattered loudly as it struck the wood.

"A moment," Lestrade said. With the ceremony completed, there remained no need to hide our presence, and so the policeman stepped from behind the trees and made his way across the soggy grounds to the burial site. Members of the family frowned upon seeing him, but quickly lost interest when it became clear he was heading past the canopy and towards the strangers. He spoke to all four, each nodding in turn.

"Clients paying their respects," said Lestrade after returning to our spot among the beeches. "I've arranged for them to come to my office tomorrow morning to claim any items of theirs that hadn't been stolen. You're invited to join us, Doctor. One never knows what someone might say. A slip up, you know."

Lestrade had offered a similar reason for attending the funeral, and nothing seemed to have come from it. Yet I agreed to the meeting as we trudged back across the wet lawn to the police van. A few moments later, the rain picked up again, but we had the shelter of the four-wheeler for protection on the long ride back to Baker Street.

*****

The lingering black clouds did not prevent my drive to Scotland Yard the following morning, and I entered Lestrade's office at precisely 11.00. It was the time he had arranged with Roderick Cheek the previous day to collect whatever of Cheek's pledges might not have been stolen from the pawnbroker. Appointments with the other clients to whom Lestrade had spoken were set at half-hour intervals thereafter. Not surprisingly, Cheek was late; and I took the opportunity to inform Lestrade of my previous meeting with the eccentric young man and his friend William Arbuthnot.

"Now?" he cried out. "You're telling me about them only now? Not yesterday at the funeral before I spoke to the two of them?"

He had a point, of course. "I was hoping to report all this to Holmes first and let him present the news. It was his Irregulars who discovered Cheek's digs, you see."

"His Irregulars? You mean those little brats Holmes puts to work? They actually found where this Roderick Cheek lives?"

"Indeed. But, you see, it was for an entirely different investigation. We were searching for a missing person. Cheek's sister came to Baker Street to ask Holmes to help her

96

find her brother who had gone missing. Holmes agreed and put the boys on the scent. His 'East End Associates,' he calls them."

Lestrade emitted a derisive snort.

Undaunted, I continued my laboured explanation. "When I learned about Cheek's dealings with Gottfried—not to mention Cheek's familiarity with Dostoevsky's novel—I suspected he might somehow be related to the current murders. His friend Arbuthnot as well."

"And you never thought to let the Yard in on your discoveries, Doctor?" asked Lestrade with the shake of his head. "I could understand Mr Holmes withholding such information, but I've always considered *you* to be much more sensible. Oh, your friend, Sherlock Holmes, has helped us on occasion, but always with a show of superiority. You, on the other hand—"

A weak knock on the door interrupted whatever compliment I might have anticipated.

"Enter!" commanded Lestrade, very much the superintendent of his tiny portion of the Metropolitan Police Headquarters.

Announcing his arrival with a cough, a bedraggled Roderick Cheek meandered into the office. William Arbuthnot, in a more appropriately appointed dark suit and waistcoat, trailed behind.

It was actually to the latter that Lestrade directed his first question. "Here, then, Mr Arbuthnot. You told me yesterday at the cemetery that you had done no business with the pawnbroker. Why have you come round?"

Arbuthnot draped an arm round Cheek's shoulder. "Moral support for my mate."

"Ah, Dr Watson," said Cheek, his rheumy eyes brightening when he recognised me, "how fitting that you are here as well. Since you are so careful a reader of *Crime and Punishment*, you should be pleased to learn that I've come to recover the only pledge of mine old Gottfried would still have had—my father's watch."

Before I could utter the words, Cheek announced them himself: "*'Just like Raskolnikov.'* Remember that he had left his father's watch with the old woman whose head he would soon be splitting open?" And Cheek slammed the edge of his right hand into the centre of his open left palm to emphasise the point. His high-pitched laugh followed the dramatic gesture.

Narrowing his eyes as he tried to interpret the meaning of this strange performance, Lestrade indicated for the two men to sit down.

"On the other hand," Cheek went right on as he sat, "unlike Raskolnikov, on my walk here"—and he held up his fingers to tick off each of the following points—"I saw no woman leaping into the Thames, no young girl being interfered with by a cold-hearted rake, and no drunken fool being run down by carriage horses. Oh, and before you ask, I also have had no dreams of some poor nag being beaten to death by its owner." Turning to Arbuthnot for approval of his wit, Cheek was rewarded with a broad grin.

I sat there with wide eyes. Cheek had just listed the most distinctive events that confront Raskolnikov in the early sections of *Crime and Punishment*. In the process, he had left me with no parallels about which to inquire.

Lestrade cleared his throat. "Tell me about this watch, then. What does it look like?"

"A silver hunter. Opens from both sides. One side is the watch face; the other contains a small portrait of my sister

Priscilla. You shouldn't have any trouble finding it, Inspector. Gottfried wrote the name of the client on the paper in which he wrapped each pledge."

Raskolnikov's pawnbroker had done the same. Nonetheless, Lestrade made a show of rummaging through a desk drawer. Perhaps he was providing additional opportunity to allow Cheek to incriminate himself. "Describe the chain, if you please," said Lestrade looking up.

Roderick Cheek's face broke into a broad grin. "You're the very devil, Inspector. Not only should the watch be wrapped in a paper with my name on it, but also—as I am sure you are aware—the watch has no chain. I pledged its steel chain to another pawnbroker a few months ago."

"Ah, yes," said Lestrade. His chicanery unmasked, he magically "discovered" the watch in question and handed it to the young man. Cheek opened both covers to be certain all was intact. Once satisfied, he signed the receipt Lestrade presented to him. The pen made a scratching sound as he wrote.

"Anything else you want to ask me?" said Cheek when he handed back the paper.

The Inspector shook his head. "That's all for now. Thanks to Dr Watson, we know where to find you."

Cheek eyed me suspiciously as Arbuthnot rose and headed for the door. Cheek was about to follow him out, but turned back to Lestrade and tugged at his forelock, a poor servant paying his respect. "Perhaps we'll see each other on Sunday," he added, and then both men were gone.

"Sunday?" I asked

"Big gathering planned for Trafalgar Square," explained Lestrade. "I should judge that all the foreign malcontents from the East End will be on hand to air their grievances. I don't doubt that this Cheek fellow will be there. Lucky not to get his skull split open. But then *our* boys restrain themselves. No axes allowed." He chuckled to himself at his little joke.

I remained in Lestrade's office for the next hour to hear what Gottfried's other two clients, the men Lestrade had cornered at the funeral, had to say; but having strong alibis for the night of the murder, they were allowed to collect their pledges and leave without any further ado.

Chapter Seven

St Petersburg

As it turned out, Sherlock Holmes had chosen a tumultuous time to be gone from London. On Sunday, 13 November, two days after Roderick Cheek's performance at Scotland Yard, an epic battle did indeed erupt in Trafalgar Square. Mounted members of the Metropolitan police along with hundreds of military troops waded into a raging sea of unemployed protesters.

So ferocious was the encounter that the resulting carnage earned the calamitous event the epithet of "Bloody Sunday." Echoing the words of Lestrade, the newspapers reported that foreign elements living in the East End—in reality, desperately poor people seeking justice—had joined the thousands of poor British workers in the Square, helping turn the affair into a riot. I assumed that if Roderick Cheek were not ill, he too was part of the mob.

I, on the contrary, was never one to side with rioters no matter how just their cause, and so I did my best to avoid the fray. That meant altering the schedule I had recently developed. During the days of Holmes' absence—that is, whenever I was free of patients—I would while away the hours at my club. Billiards, newspapers, conversation, the odd glass of Guinness—all served to address my needs. On the day scheduled for the mass protest, however, I decided to forego such pleasures. On that particular Sunday, I stayed clear of central London.

For his part, Lestrade had his hands full. At the same time he was wrestling with the Brick Lane murders, he also had to help sort out the angry workers who had been arrested and brought to the Yard.

Not to say that Holmes and I did not face our own challenges with two investigations going on at the same time. As yet, we had not reached any tangible conclusions regarding the murders of Gottfried and his wife though, thanks to the Irregulars, I considered closed the case that dealt with the whereabouts of Roderick Cheek. Oh, I could have informed Miss Cheek of our success myself; but as the lady was Holmes' client, I assumed that, just as I had told Lestrade concerning my interviews with Cheek and Arbuthnot, Holmes would attend to the matter upon his return.

Speaking of Holmes, I should mention that in spite of the length of his absence, I worried little about not having heard from him. I understood that his work took him to many strange places—though I must confess that I did indeed wonder what he might be up to.

Late Wednesday afternoon, the eighth day since Holmes' departure, the answer finally came. Upon returning to Baker Street following an afternoon at my club, I was happily surprised to discover my friend ensconced in our sitting room. I can picture him today as he struck one of his favourite attitudes, sitting cross-legged in an armchair enjoying his favourite briar before the hearth. It was as if he had never been away.

"Holmes!" I fairly shouted. "You've come back!"

"Ah, Watson," said he directing a cloud of blue smoke heavenward, "I underestimate your powers of observation. As you have so astutely noted, I have indeed 'come back.' Fix us a brandy and water, and I shall report to you my adventures."

I hung my mac and bowler on the pegs near the door and, after preparing us both a brandy with water from the gasogene, settled into the armchair next to Holmes.

"Where have you been?" I asked.

"Why, to St Petersburg, old fellow, the capital of the Russian empire. On the Gottfried case. I thought that was obvious. That is why I didn't think to tell you."

St Petersburg once more.

However insensitive his reasoning, I was most pleased at the news. Holmes' long journey to St Petersburg could not have been better proof of his faith in my interpretation of Dostoevsky's novel. As for undertaking a trip to Russia in the first place, the enterprise did not surprise me. After all, as I would report in my sketch concerning Irene Adler, earlier that same year he had already travelled to Odessa to help the local authorities solve the infamous Trepoff murder.

Though Odessa lies to the south and St Petersburg to the north, a look at a map will show that the two Russian cities are similar in distance from London. In point of fact, both of Holmes' excursions began in the same manner—a London train to Queenborough on the Isle of Sheppey in Kent and a night boat to Flushing on the coast of Holland. It was in

Holland that the trips diverged; Holmes made the railway journey south to Odessa in the winter and the trip north to St Petersburg in the fall. In both cases, he went prepared for cold weather.

More significant is that he returned from the latter excursion with kind words for me. "I owe you a grand apology, Watson," he said, gesturing with his pipe in my direction.

"Thank you, Holmes. You are most kind. But for what exactly are you apologizing?"

Holmes emitted more smoke in a long exhalation. When he was finished, he said, "You are to be complimented for recognizing the motivation of the Gottfried murders." He lifted his glass. "To Watson and his literary insights," he toasted. "Long may they reign." Then he sipped the brandy in my honour.

I smiled broadly in response.

"First," said Holmes, "allow me to admit that as soon as you pointed out the parallels between Gottfried's murder and that of the pawnbroker in *Crime and Punishment*, I suspected you were on to something. Needless to say, my own view of the crime paralleled Dostoevsky's account from the start."

"Really, Holmes," I bristled. "I would not have guessed."

"Oh, yes. But in order to maintain an objective investigation, I needed to remain uncommitted. Before I dared confirm your enthusiastic embrace of Dostoevsky's plot, I wanted a first-hand account of what had transpired in Petersburg twenty years before. Hence, my trip. And now I am convinced."

Better late than never.

"You were quite right, old fellow. There can be no doubt that the murders in Petersburg were the catalyst for the crimes here in London."

"I knew it!"

"Yes, but allow me to go a step farther. I trust that you recall the actual murders I described that may have influenced Dostoevsky."

I nodded dutifully.

"Well, consider this. Twenty years ago, might not some wretched contemporary of Dostoevsky been similarly inspired—that is, *criminally* inspired? What if just such a villain—let us call him Raskolnikov as Dostoevsky did—was living in St Petersburg at the time and acting out an earlier crime. That is, what if the miscreant himself was copying one of those murders from the past?"

"What are you saying, Holmes?" Now it was my turn to sample the brandy. I had never thought to look at the St Petersburg murders from such a perspective. But then why should I? "The crimes described by Dostoevsky were fiction," I reminded him.

"Watson," said he with a smile of anticipation, "consider the proposition that up to the point at which the murderer confesses, *Crime and Punishment* is a factual account of two real killings. I suggest that the two murders you just referred to as 'fictional' are, in truth, actual events that Dostoevsky disguised only slightly, events that occurred within the year before his book began appearing in serial publication."

"You can't be serious, Holmes. Dostoevsky is a novelist, not a reporter. Unlike myself who described actual murders in *A Study in Scarlet*, he had to conjure his crimes from within his own imagination. Oh, the narrative may have been inspired by some of those true cases you mentioned, but—"

Holmes cut me off. "Have I ever spoken to you of my friend in the Petersburg detective bureau? I first encountered him a few months before you and I met. He helped me solve the theft of a valuable stone from the Langham, the Garibaldi Diamond. The culprit had absconded to Petersburg; and thanks to this fellow, I was able to track him down."

I was still wrestling with the idea that Dostoevsky had written an account of two actual murders. Picturing a Russian detective whom Holmes had befriended posed a less difficult challenge.

"I never thought to inform you that once we had settled the murders connected to Lauriston Gardens, I cabled the police in Petersburg. My friend on the force confirmed for me what the world will soon discover with the publication of *A Study in Scarlet*—that it was indeed from Petersburg that Jefferson Hope, just as he reported to us, had left for Paris on the trail of Drebber and Stangerson."

"I had no idea you contacted the Russian police."

"I could offer you my friend's real name," Holmes said, "but I should imagine you would like to employ the appellation bestowed upon him by Dostoevsky. After all, it was Dostoevsky who dramatised his most celebrated case, Raskolnikov's axe murders."[7]

"Not Porfiry Petrovitch!" I cried out. "Why, I remember him from the book."

"Exactly, old fellow! Porfiry Petrovitch was thirty-five when he arrested Raskolnikov for those killings. He is now sixty-six—still short, plump, and balding. Perhaps even a little more so in all three areas."

"Then to Porfiry," I said, raising my glass.

"Porfiry *Petrovitch*," Holmes corrected. "The Russians do love their patronymics."

"To Porfiry *Petrovitch* then," and the two of us finished our brandies.

"Porfiry is very different from me, Watson," said Holmes, already disregarding the patronymic in the name of friendship. "You know my methods. I rely on facts. He

---

[7] All the key Russian names in this narrative were invented by Dostoevsky for *Crime and Punishment*. It should be noted that in the serialization of the novel, the *actual* identity of the murderer was never made public. To facilitate keeping track of him, however, I, like Dostoevsky, have employed the same fictional name for the man from beginning to end— Raskolnikov. (JHW)

believes that facts are the very details that lead one to false conclusions. No, for Porfiry Petrovitch, psychology is the thing. He ensnares his prey with a wink and a smile. Why, without revealing an ounce of evidence—evidence he claimed to possess—he predicted to Raskolnikov that the man's psychological nature would drive him to confess. And the villain soon did."

"Marvellous."

"Indeed," said Holmes. "Though Porfiry's manner of doing things is not my own, I never hesitate to call on the man for help.[8] On this last occasion, I met him in his office at the station house, a pale-yellow building fronted with greying white pilasters and cornices. It was particularly cold the day I arrived—close to freezing, in fact—and I was happy to go inside.

"The police bureau is a network of small offices on the fourth floor, and to reach it I had to climb a steep set of stairs

---

[8] Some seven years later, Holmes would cable Porfiry Petrovitch regarding the investigation I titled "The Golden Pince-Nez". It was from the Russian detective that Holmes gained background regarding the Russian Nihilist organization of which Professor Coram had once been a member. (JHW)

teeming with all manner of people—not only official clerks and uniformed police, but also the wretches who live in the numerous flats on the lower floors. Porfiry's digs are attached to his office. In fact, he likes to joke that his flat is not unlike a prison-cell since both are funded by the government."

"A wry sense of humour," I noted, "especially for a policeman."

"Just so. In that part of the city I fancy it stands him in good stead. The area remains one of the most squalid and violent parts of Petersburg. And yet, though Porfiry knew I wanted to see the lodging house that Raskolnikov occupied at the time of the murders—in fact, only a quarter-mile from the police station—my friend had too much pride in his city not to take a detour to point out the sights. Standing at a railing by the Neva, we gazed at the lengthy green-and-white façade of the Winter Palace and the stately mansions and manicured gardens along the *Promenade des Anglais*, the so-called English Embankment, further west."

"Sounds beautiful," I said.

"True, Watson, but like all great metropolises, Petersburg is a city of contrasts; and just minutes after showing off the magisterial residence of the Tsars, Porfiry Petrovitch was guiding me through the chaotic Haymarket to Raskolnikov's shabby neighbourhood. Raskolnikov lived near Stoliarny Place not far from the Kokushkin Bridge that spans a foul-smelling canal south of the river.

"From Raskolnikov's run-down, yellow-brick building, we marched fewer than a thousand paces—Dostoevsky numbers them at seven hundred thirty—to the site of the axe murders themselves, a building of greyish-yellow colour in Srednaya Podyacheskaya Street on the other side of the small Voznesensky Bridge."

I stared blankly at the growing list of awkward-sounding names.

"No matter the specific locations today," said Holmes with a dismissive wave, "since none of the major players, with the exception of Porfiry Petrovitch himself, lives there anymore. Yet he says the whole area looks much as it did twenty years ago.

"The nearby Haymarket is still known as the underbelly of the city; and with its wild assortment of costermongers, beggars, and livestock, it is quite the hurly-burly. A group of erstwhile musicians with concertina and tambourines produced discordant sounds in the hope of raising money, and drunks staggering about joined in song. And the smells! —the animal waste, the rotten food, the sweat of humanity. I tell you, Watson, it is not unlike some Byzantine bazaar. Think of our own Spitalfields Market."

I understood Holmes' reference to the raucous marketplace in the East End, but somehow the turmoil of a Russian setting swarming with foreigners seemed much coarser than any British scene I could conjure.

"Let us also not forget," said he, "the taverns, brothels, and dosshouses that one expects to find adjacent to any such vanity fair. I should fancy that the prostitutes with their yellow tickets of legality are quite adept at catering to the workers and farmers and thieves who frequent the place. Is it any wonder that Dostoevsky's murderer believed he could escape detection in such an atmosphere?"

I nodded my head at the obvious.

"You do realize," said Holmes, pointing the stem of his pipe in my direction, "that at some point Dostoevsky actually lived not far from where the murders in the novel occurred, a fact that speaks for the book's authenticity. Because Dostoevsky's rooms were also near the police station, it was as a neighbour that he came to know Porfiry Petrovitch and from the detective himself that he acquired the gruesome details he recreated in his novel, details he sought to publish as quickly as possible."

With the publication of my own work coming so soon, I could well understand Dostoevsky's eagerness.

"Porfiry Petrovitch," he continued, "brought me to a tavern that Raskolnikov had visited, a rundown place called the Crystal Palace. We were lucky enough to secure seating in one of the cleaner rooms. Porfiry himself used to go there with Dostoevsky."

"And how was the famous Russian vodka?" I could not refrain from asking.

Holmes smiled. "We drank tea, old fellow. Porfiry does not drink spirits."

"Tea in the Crystal Palace—how very English," I mused though I could picture no resemblance between the shabby establishment described by Holmes and the original Crystal Palace, the grand structure of glass and iron built in Hyde Park for the Great Exhibition of 1851. "One fancies the name is ironical," I hastened to add. (Underscoring such irony, Mrs Garnett named the tavern in French, *Palais de Cristal*.)

In point of fact, on not a few occasions, Holmes and I might be seen in south London, witnessing summer fireworks in the Palace's relocated home in Sydenham. With scientific displays from all parts of the Empire, the original Crystal Palace symbolised the progress of modern technology. (Strangely, as many times as Holmes and I had visited the place, I could never seem to identify the location of the clock chimes which I still maintain ring somewhere within its glass walls.)[9]

"Ironical, to be sure," said Holmes. "Porfiry Petrovitch said that the Russian Socialists hated the English Palace because it reflected the lockstep mentality forced upon the working class. But we are getting far afield, old fellow. In terms of the old axe murders that I came to investigate, it was in that tavern that Raskolnikov captured the interest of the local authorities. Remember how he told a police clerk just

---

[9] Because no such chimes have been shown to exist, Watson's insistence remains a point of controversy ever since he first mentioned hearing them in *The Sign of Four*. One alternative for the source is the tower clock in the Royal Normal College for the Blind in nearby Upper Norwood. For Watson's reference to the school itself, see "An Adventure in Darkness" (which I edited) in *Sherlock Holmes Adventures in the Realms of HG Wells* published by Belanger Books. (DDV)

how he, Raskolnikov, would have performed the murders if he was the one who had killed the pawnbroker."

I remembered, and yet I remained sceptical. "In spite of all that you are reporting and all the various locations you have visited, Holmes, St Petersburg still seems a great distance to have travelled in order to witness the scene of a twenty-year-old crime."

"Crimes, Watson, crimes. There were *two* murders, let us not forget—those of the pawnbroker called Ayona Ivanovna and her sister Lizaveta. But to your point, I wanted information that I suspected the Petersburg police might still have. Recall that towards the end of the investigation, Porfiry Petrovitch told Raskolnikov that the police possessed absolute proof of who had killed the pawnbroker."

"Yes," I remembered, "but Porfiry Petrovitch tells Raskolnikov that he will not reveal the proof since he wants the killer to confess without the coercion of inculpatory evidence."

Holmes paused and held up a forefinger. "A moment."

Only then did I notice his Gladstone, which was leaning against his chair.

Putting down his pipe, he withdrew from inside the bag a copy of Whishaw's translation of *Crime and Punishment*. (I did not know he owned one.) "I call your attention," said he as he thumbed through the pages, "to Porfiry Petrovitch's climactic interview with Raskolnikov." And coming to a stop near the end, he proceeded to read the Russian detective's remarks to the killer: "'I hold a proof . . . . God has sent it to me.'" (Mrs Garnett would call it "a little fact" sent by "Providence.") "Just as you or I might respond when confronted with such a statement, Watson, Raskolnikov rightly asked, 'What is it?'"

In light of the fact that Dostoevsky himself never revealed this evidence, I myself entertained the very same question.

"In order to understand more about the murders," Holmes smiled, "I asked Porfiry Petrovitch the nature of this evidence. His answer?" Here Sherlock Holmes, never one to overlook the chance to display his acting talents, evoked a Russian accent. "'Iss information, Mr Holmes, I hold secret a little longer. As you English say, I shall keep it 'close to the chest.'"

I chuckled in spite of myself.

"You see," said Holmes, "from the start, Porfiry Petrovitch wanted Raskolnikov to turn himself in and acknowledge the crime on his own." (Mrs Garnett would write, "surrender and confess.") "Presenting him with incriminating evidence might have coerced an admission of guilt, but Porfiry was seeking a freely offered confession. Which, as we know from the novel, the villain ultimately did provide, earning him—as Porfiry had predicted—a lesser sentence—ten years in Siberia rather than a lifetime."

"I thought it was eight," I said with a frown. "The epilogue provides the number."

Holmes shook his head. "Remember that Dostoevsky sought to finish the novel as quickly as he could—in point of fact, just after Raskolnikov's confession. What Dostoevsky wrote following the confession is mere conjecture. Oh, the epilogue is based on the facts Raskolnikov gave to the police, and yet Dostoevsky imagined it all. Some of it—like the death of Raskolnikov's mother—he got right, but the eight-year sentence? Simply an incorrect guess."

As a writer myself, I remembered sensing stylistic differences between the epilogue and the earlier text. In the epilogue, there is much narrative but little dialogue, much description but little drama. Yet even as I could understand Dostoevsky's need for haste in making public the story, I could not comprehend the shortness of Raskolnikov's imprisonment.

"Eight years or ten, Holmes—either way, it is too short a time for killing two women. Here in England he would have hanged."

"True, Watson. The court showed mercy. But remember that by turning himself in, Raskolnikov saved the state much legal work and exonerated the poor soul who had confessed to the murders untruthfully."

"The house-painter Nikolay," I said, "the man who found the dropped earrings and for his troubles was accused of the crime."

"And falsely confessed. Just so. And do not forget the family and friends of Raskolnikov who spoke to the positive history of the killer—how kind he had been to others, how he had rescued people in a fire—not to mention the travails of his childhood." Holmes closed the book.

"Two sides to the man," I recalled, "the *homo duplex* to which you referred at the Gottfried murder scene."

"Exactly, Watson. Raskolnikov had a double nature—or so Porfiry Petrovitch believed. Raskolnikov could be full of compassion on the one hand and cold and ruthless on the other, both emotional and calculating, full of sympathy and full of self-loathing.

"Truth be told, Porfiry Petrovitch confessed to me that he thought Raskolnikov had listened less to the police and more to Sofya Semyonovna Marmeladov, the God-fearing woman Raskolnikov called Sonia and with whom he was destined to fall in love. It was the devoted Sonia, not himself, that Porfiry Petrovitch believed to be the prime mover in getting Raskolnikov to surrender."

"A most interesting fellow, your Russian policeman."

"True, Watson, but then you and I are in the midst of our own murder case, not one already solved twenty years ago."

So infatuated had I become with hearing about Dostoevsky's machinations in producing *Crime and Punishment* that I had almost forgotten all that I had learned when Holmes was gone. My friend was correct; it was time to return to the present, which, of course, was also connected to the past.

"Regarding the Gottfried case, Holmes, I'm afraid it has more to do with the twenty-year old murders than you have already reported." And I proceeded to tell him of the informer Lestrade had called the Assistant.

Holmes steepled his fingers beneath his chin. "The Assistant, you say?"

I nodded yes.

"These are deep waters indeed," he replied. "Do you not remember Dostoevsky's account of Raskolnikov's confession?"

Of course! Now I recalled what the Assistant had failed to mention when Lestrade brought him to Baker Street. "Raskolnikov offered his confession to a hot-headed police assistant!" I cried. "According to Whishaw, people named him 'Explosive.' The man told Lestrade and me that he was called Dmitry."

"Pure fabrication. His real name is Ilya Petrovitch Poruchik though he sometimes calls himself Alexsandr Ilich."

"I do not remember—"

"You will not find those names in the novel proper, Watson, but both appear in Dostoevsky's notebooks. Porfiry Petrovitch showed them to me—pages and pages filled with comments on the case, all written in excellent penmanship, precise and slanted"—he used his hand to show the angle just past the vertical—"yet also a bit maddening with their share of cross-outs and inserts. Sometimes he wrote sideways in the margins; sometimes, even upside-down. And—oh, yes—one cannot forget the drawings—figures, faces, churches. The whole business is something to behold."

I could only imagine! What a trove of information! Little wonder that Holmes knew so much more than I about Ilya Petrovitch.

"Lestrade told me about the Assistant's anger," I said. "The man's hostility so aroused the ire of his colleagues that they had him dismissed from the force."

"Actually, it was Porfiry himself who dismissed him."

"And now," I observed, "we discover that this informer for Lestrade actually played a significant role in the old case in St Petersburg. You should know, Holmes, that Ilya Petrovitch dismissed any such similarities as 'coincidence'."

Holmes chuckled dryly. "As I am sure you are aware, Watson, I do not believe in coincidence."

Returning to our brandies, we both sat quietly for a few minutes. When Holmes spoke again, it was to change the subject—except, of course, it was really the same subject.

"Regarding the other investigation in which we find ourselves entangled," he asked, "what can you tell me of Roderick Cheek? I should like to hear more about his circumstances before I contact his sister."

How Holmes already knew about my meeting with the young man I could only guess. Presumably, he had got the information from Charlie Duffle before returning to Baker Street. Whatever the case, I reported to Holmes all I had learned about the strange brother of the woman who had asked us to find him—and the even stranger connection he seemed to have with the decades-old Russian murders. For good measure, I added what I knew of Cheek's friend Arbuthnot.

"Well done, Watson," Holmes reassured me. Relighting his pipe, he added, "On the morrow I should like to visit the lodgings of Roderick Cheek myself." Then he inhaled deeply and closed his eyes. Within moments, small wisps of smoke began escaping from the corners of his lips and making their journey upward, dissipating before ever reaching the ceiling.

Chapter Eight
The *Fiancé*

And so once more unto the East End. Yet again the hansom driver required extra coins to take us there. Yet again the choking traffic, the muddied roads, the raucous cries, the powerful stench. Holmes absorbed everything without a murmur; but when we finally arrived in front of the Lindermann shop that Thursday afternoon, I was more than ready—stink and all—for the relative quiet within the boarding house.

We climbed the stairs; and upon reaching Cheek's fourth-storey room, I delivered a sharp rap on the door. Receiving no response, I knocked again only harder. This time we were rewarded not by any sounds from within, but from the door itself, obviously unlocked, which—as during my previous visit—slowly creaked open.

"Saves me the trouble," Holmes murmured, patting the coat pocket where he stowed his small jemmy tools.

"Holmes, you don't mean to say you intend to enter?"

"Of course I do, Watson. The door is not locked."

"But you—"

He walked into the room before I could accuse him of breaking the law.

All was as it had been on my first visit in the tiny quarters, save for the pile of blankets on the bed. On this occasion, no one was under them; and yet they appeared even more haphazardly thrown together—if such a display could be contemplated.

For his part, Holmes circled the perimeter of the small confines using the toe of his boot to test for weaknesses in the baseboard just below where the yellowed wallpaper ended. It was in such an opening that Raskolnikov had initially hidden the gold trinkets he had stolen from the murdered pawnbroker.

Holmes next turned his attention to the drawers, pulling them out to have a look, then proceeding to examine the bookshelf. On the top, a few handwritten sheets of paper lay fastened together. Holmes quickly read through the pages and then showed them to me. Someone had translated into English

Raskolnikov's article on crime that had appeared in the Russian pamphlet called *Periodical Word* (Mrs Garnett translated the title as *Periodical Review*.) It was the same article that had so fascinated Porfiry Petrovitch in *Crime and Punishment*.

In it, Raskolnikov argued that the great men of history, the extraordinary men, got, as it were, a "free pass" to ignore the laws set out for the rest of us, the ordinary, inferior people of the world. ("The law is not for them," as Mrs Garnett succinctly rendered it.) If necessary to further their own important goals, the great men—Napoleon or Isaac Newton, to cite but two of Raskolnikov's examples—should be allowed to commit murder. For where would the world be without their notable accomplishments?

According to Holmes, it was Porfiry Petrovitch's belief throughout the investigation that Raskolnikov placed himself on a level with those extraordinary men. As a matter of course, it followed that Raskolnikov viewed the pawnbroker he murdered as nothing more than a louse.

Suddenly, we heard loud voices and a heavy tramp of feet coming down the corridor. I replaced the papers just as the door opened; and Roderick Cheek, obviously aware that uninvited people were in his room, put only his head in to have a safe look-round. When he saw my familiar face, he pushed the door wide open, strutted in, and waved for his companion, William Arbuthnot, to join him.

"Well, well, well," he trumpeted, "what do we have here? Two robbers in need of a police escort to the clink? What do you propose, William? You're reading for the law."

Holmes and I stood our ground. We had not been caught riffling through Cheek's drawers, after all; and one cannot forget that the door had been left unlocked.

"My name is Sherlock Holmes," announced my friend, "and I am working with the police to help solve the mystery of the murdered pawnbroker."

"Ah, yes," said Cheek, "back to Dostoevsky."

"Have you searched the room for the hole in the wall yet," William wanted to know, "the hidey where Raskolnikov first stashed the stolen jewellery?"

Holmes and I exchanged glances. It was obvious that William too recalled the details of the crime in the novel.

"And don't forget," added William, "that Raskolnikov had a sister who wanted to marry an unctuous cad just to gain money to help her brother."

"Like Priscilla," snarled Roderick. "Except that I haven't convinced her not to do so just yet."

"Her *fiancé*, Percy Farragut, is a banker," said William. "Swells like him favour women who lack their own funds— just like that ass Luzhin in *Crime and Punishment*, who wanted to marry Raskolnikov's sister. A woman's poor provenance enables these toffs to act as lord-and-master. Priscilla is a case in point."

"Farragut's a swine," muttered Roderick. Then he blurted out some more of that high-pitched laughter before adding, "Maybe some foul play will come his way."

"I don't know about that," said William, "but I do know that your sister deserves better than Percy 'bloody' Farragut. Why, his only attraction is his money! I can tell you that if I had the funds that he does, I would be pursuing Priscilla myself."

"You and my sister?" laughed Roderick. "Don't be daft." And together the two of them broke into a cascade of silly laughter—just what one might expect from a pair of inebriated university students. Save that Roderick no longer attended, and neither one appeared drunk.

"Come, Watson," said Holmes. "There's nothing more to be learned from these two." With a quick nod of his head that did nothing to interrupt the young men's jollity, Holmes exited the room, and I followed.

On our way out to the street, I insisted we stop in at Lindermann's. Since first seeing the food shop more than a week before, I had developed a craving for *halva*, the honey-and-sesame-based confection, which I had discovered during my military service in Afghanistan. Hoping it would be available among the Jewish foods as well, I was pleased to discover that this turned out to be the case. Holmes turned down the portion I offered him in the hansom, and so I feasted by myself on the large, marbled chunk I had purchased for the two of us. It lasted for most of our drive back to Baker Street.

*****

We arrived in our sitting room that Thursday afternoon to discover a thin, balding man in a smart though tight-fitting grey suit postured primly on our settee. He wore a Vandyke beard and peered up at us through a *pince-nez* clipped to the bridge of his nose. A black bowler perched on his right knee.

"Mr Farragut, I presume," said Holmes, "how good of you to come calling."

Why, we had just been discussing the *fiancé* of Miss Priscilla Cheek, and here sat that very personage. The man stood, his furrowed brow indicating how bewildered he was at being identified so easily. The bowler rolled to the floor.

"But how—?"

"Tosh, man," said Holmes. "Your card lay in the brass platter downstairs just inside the outer door. It is where our landlady always places such items when she has allowed someone to wait for us."

"Oh, yes," said he, stooping to pick up his hat. She did escort me up here. In fact, she kept quite the eye on me. Afraid I might upset some of your precious belongings, I shouldn't doubt."

Presumptuous prig, I surprised myself by concluding on such short notice. *Certainly not an appropriate suitor for a sensitive young lady like Miss Cheek.* I had only just met the man, and yet I had taken an immediate dislike to him—even with the knowledge that such an attitude put me in the same singular camp as her brother and William Arbuthnot.

Holmes seemed equally put off. How else to interpret the impatience in his tone? "Now that you can see I am no clairvoyant, Mr Farragut, you will understand that I have no way of divining the purpose of your visit. Dr Watson and I are in the midst of helping the police investigate a pair of brutal murders, and I suggest you tell us the nature of your business so we may go about pursuing our work."

Unruffled by Holmes' directness, the man announced, "I am here to personally invite you gentlemen to join my *fiancée*, Miss Priscilla Cheek, and me for dinner tomorrow evening. I know she has been here to speak to you about her brother; and since my 'business,' as you so aptly put it, deals with the two of them, I thought a person like yourself, Mr Holmes, whom Miss Cheek obviously trusts, should be there to witness the terms I intend to put before her."

"Terms?" I repeated, my sense of gallantry offended. "*Terms* for your intended? Certainly, Mr Farragut, this is no way to begin a lifelong relationship—especially not with so clearly fair-minded a young lady as Miss Cheek."

Holmes allowed himself a quick smile at my remark before accepting the invitation. "Where and when, Mr

Farragut? I believe I speak for Dr Watson when I say we both eagerly anticipate hearing what you have to say."

"We shall meet at Simpson's tomorrow evening at 8," Farragut announced. "I have booked a private room upstairs. I suppose it only fair to tell you that Miss Cheek wanted her brother to be present as well. I quashed the suggestion, of course. I have no use for the vagabond, and I told her so. More of this we shall discuss tomorrow evening."

With those final words, Farragut rose, leaned forward in a kind of farewell bow, and departed.

"One wonders," Holmes observed after we heard the outer door close, "if this fellow would have extended us the invitation had he known we consider Miss Cheek's brother a possible suspect in a murder case."

Had the matter not been so grave, I might have categorised that look in the steel-grey eyes of Sherlock Holmes as a twinkle.

*****

Though fall weather continued to chill the city that Friday, Holmes and I deemed the evening warm enough for an invigorating walk to the Strand. Simpson's was always a desired destination. With its wood-panelled walls, marble floors, and rich-textured carpeting, the ambiance of its interior could almost make one believe that the restaurant was the centre of the Empire.

Holmes and I arrived minutes before the arranged meeting-time and found Farragut and Miss Cheek waiting for us in the entryway. We ascended the stairs to the intimate room Farragut had hired and in a matter of minutes were seated before the establishment's whitest linen, finest china, and most sparkling flatware.

"A pre-prandial aperitif?" Farragut offered.

It took the stomp of rapid footfalls on the nearby staircase but a moment to destroy the tranquillity. Seconds later, none other than the lady's twin, a winded Mr Roderick Cheek, arrived at our table. Dressed in a well-worn grey coat, he kept it wrapped about himself when he grabbed a chair from next to the wall and, squeezing it between Miss Cheek and Holmes, collapsed onto the seat.

The panting *maître d'*, who had come scurrying up the stairs behind young Cheek, hastened into our little room, obviously too astonished by the young man's quick entrance to have kept him out.

"Is there a problem, Mr Farragut?" the *maître d'* asked, still breathing heavily.

Before Farragut could utter a word, Miss Cheek spoke up. "Everything's quite all right. I invited this man myself."

The *maître d'* rose to his full height, which in truth was not so grand, eyed Roderick's threadbare coat with disdain, and then huffed his way out the door and back down the stairs.

Now it was the waiter's turn to approach our table, but Farragut waved him away. Rather, he addressed himself to Miss Cheek. "I specifically ordered you *not* to invite your brother to this engagement."

"Ordered"? Has this fellow no sense of boundaries?

"You also said you that wished to speak to me about him, Percy," replied Miss Cheek calmly, "and I saw no reason why he should not be present to hear what you have to say. After all, to marry me is to marry into my family."

Roderick's eyes burned with fever as he listened to the exchange. Sick as he appeared to be, I wondered if the man might nonetheless be capable of inflicting bodily harm upon Farragut. A silver trolley off to the side was filled with joints of beef waiting to be carved. I knew it also maintained a fine selection of the finest blades. Not counting the occasional cough, however, all Cheek actually did was to continue sitting quietly.

"Well then, Priscilla," said Farragut. "Let me say it to you clearly. In fact, I invited Mr Holmes and Dr Watson for dinner to serve as witnesses. I did not want your brother here tonight, and I forbid you from seeing him once we are married. It is a condition of our nuptials—you must choose between him and me. Him *or* me."

The young woman patted the back of her brother's hand and then took hold of it. "I'm sorry you feel so antagonistic towards Roderick, Percy; but you must never ask a sister to disown her brother, especially not her twin."

Miss Cheek's loyalty obviously stimulated her brother. Ill or not, he directed his remark to Farragut. "She only wanted to marry you for *my* sake," he proclaimed. "She hoped to get enough money from you, old man, to help return me to the study of law. She has never loved you—as if anyone ever could."

After a moment of awful silence, Percy Farragut picked up his white serviette. Although he had eaten nothing at table, he blotted his lips, and rising dramatically, addressed the following words to Miss Cheek: "I was hoping you would see things *my* way, Priscilla; but since you have not, then I must wish you good evening." He took a step in the direction of the exit and paused. Turning round to face her once more, he added, "Good-bye, actually." And then he was gone.

Where—or if—the murder of the Gottfrieds fit into this family drama I did not know. I can only say that I was happy to see the back of Percy Farragut. For a moment, the four of us sat quietly though I did cast a surreptitious glance at Miss Cheek and her brother to determine if they—she in particular—seemed content with Farragut's departure. I was rewarded with the sight of their hands clasping as Roderick placed a kiss on his sister's cheek.

"I won't stay, Pris," muttered Roderick. "I just wanted to hear you say the right thing." He pushed back his chair, stood up; and then he too, albeit slowly, exited the room. How he had got himself from Goulston Street to the Strand that night and then back again I never learned.

"Under the circumstances, gentlemen," said Miss Cheek, "I hope you will forgive me for desiring to leave as well. I've had quite a shock this evening."

"Of course," said I, speaking for Holmes. "I shall see you to a cab." Yet to my friend I whispered, "I say, Holmes, let us not allow this private room to go to waste. I propose that we enjoy the bill of fare upon my return."

I escorted Miss Cheek downstairs and through the restaurant. Once outside I was able to hail her a hansom. When I returned to the table, I was pleased to see Holmes in negotiations with the white-suited carver who manned the silver trolley. A savoury cut of beef appeared to be the topic of discussion.

Chapter Nine

Incognito

In spite of the nagging chill, the night had remained warm enough for Holmes and me to walk the two miles back to Baker Street. There were not many people about, and spotting the Orthodox Jew who seemed to be following us required no great skills of detection.

He was attired in a wide-brimmed, black top hat beneath which his brown side locks spiralled downward like a pair of oversized corkscrews. In traditional long black coat and white stockings, he was difficult not to notice. Such a figure might go unmarked in the Old Jewry section of the city, but in the Strand he could not be missed.

I knew that Friday nights marked the onset of the Jewish Sabbath; but as far as I was aware, there was no admonition against walking in one's own neighbourhood. Whilst the man followed us along Shaftesbury Avenue and then into St Giles High Street, I said nothing to Holmes. But when he made the turn into Oxford Street moments after we had, I asked Holmes if he had noticed him as well.

"The chap with the black hat, Watson? If you are referring to the same person who watched us enter Simpson's and who has been trailing us ever since we left the restaurant, then, yes, old fellow, I am indeed aware of him. Take no notice. We shall find out his business in due time."

It was close to 11 when we reached Baker Street and just a few minutes later when we entered our sitting room. No sooner had we removed our coats than an obviously disturbed Mrs Hudson knocked at our door. "There is—" she searched for the appropriate word "— a *person* to see you, Mr Holmes. It is rather late and I—"

His quick response surprised me. "That's all right, Mrs Hudson. I know the gentleman in question. Please show him in."

With the same disdainful eye she reserved for anyone she failed to regard as "English," Mrs Hudson opened wide the door and allowed into our sitting room the same Jewish fellow who had been following us all evening. With a slow shake of her head, she then disappeared. As for our visitor, a plump little man with a sallow complexion, in spite of his unique haberdashery, what most stood out was the hint of merriment in his frequently blinking eyes.

I was about to wish him a "Good Sabbath," as I believe is the Friday-night custom among Jewish people, when Holmes sprang up to shake his hand. But much to my surprise—and, I might add, to my friend's discomfort—not only did the stranger embrace him but also planted kisses on each of Holmes' cheeks. It was then I began to suspect that the figure before me, apparently already recognised by Holmes, was not as spiritual as he was disguised to appear.

"Watson," said Holmes after breaking free from the visitor's arms, "may I present to you a man of many disguises. Mr Porfiry Petrovitch, the grand investigator from St Petersburg. Like me, when the situation presents itself, he cannot resist making a dramatic entrance."

I remembered Porfiry Petrovitch's disguise when he hounded Raskolnikov. In greasy hat and great long coat, he rattled the suspect by anonymously addressing him as "murderer." This evening he was at it again—only this time, just as I had contemplated at the Gottfried's funeral, in religious garb.

In salutation, the Orthodox Jew—though now I knew he was anything but—doffed not only his top hat but also the tangles of dark-brown hair attached to it, and bowed in my direction. As he leaned forward, his bald crown fringed in grey reflected the light. It was, as Dostoevsky rightly described, a head too large for the man's short, round frame.

"Iss pleasure to meet you, Doctor," said he extending a hand. "Holmes has told me much about you, and I look forward to reading the account he tells me is coming soon."

"*A Study in Scarlet*," I said proudly. "In a Christmas magazine due to be published in just a few days—Monday, in fact." Not only did the man know how to charm, he could do so in serviceable English.

"Shall we mark the occasion with a glass of port?" I asked.

Porfiry Petrovitch raised his hand. "Not for me. Alcohol is not to my taste." Indeed, I remembered hearing of the tea he and Holmes had enjoyed in St Petersburg. "Permit me to enjoy my vice," the Russian added, "cigarettes."

I was about to offer him one my own—from Bradley of Oxford Street—but with a sheepish smile, he reached inside his black coat and produced a small package. "For years,

144

doctor tell me, stop." Holding up an ill-shaped, dark-papered cigarette, he said, "You see result—heh, heh, heh. *Makhorka.* I—how to say? —roll them myself."

Holmes offered Porfiry Petrovitch a box of Vestas, and we seated ourselves before the fire as the Russian struck a match. "Watson," said Holmes "you and I shall have the wine if Porfiry does not object."

With a nod and a smile, our guest offered his encouragement, and I filled two small glasses with dark-red port for Holmes and me. In spite of the foul-smelling cigarette smoke clouding the room, the three of us made quite the congenial group. It would be difficult for an outsider to discern that we were in the middle of an investigation involving two murderous attacks with an axe.

As he inhaled, Porfiry Petrovitch closed his eyes. Almost immediately, however, he opened them again. "I forget apology, gentlemen," said he. "Please, forgive the disguise. Iss better if people do not know I am yet in London."

"Not to worry," said Holmes. "Your rooms are sufficient?"

"*Spasiba.* Thank you."

"*Puzhalsta*," Holmes replied in the strange Russian tongue. Until now, I had not a clue that he understood a word of the inscrutable language, let alone the ability to speak it. "The accommodations are suitable for the two of you?" he added.

"*Da.* Yes."

"Porfiry is travelling with a—a friend," Holmes explained to me. "I secured rooms for them in Montague Street near my old flat. He wanted to tour the British Museum."

"I go today—in afternoon," he said, eyes blinking. "I see Elgin Marbles and Egyptian mummies. Most satisfying." He emphasised the pleasure with a long pull on his cigarette.

"Excellent choices," said I. "But, Holmes, you never informed me that your friend was coming to London."

Holmes sampled his port. "Though I arranged his rooms, I did not know for certain he would actually get here until I recognised him outside of Simpson's. But here he most certainly is. And I should imagine that as the chief investigator of those pawnbroker murders in St Petersburg twenty years ago, he can enlighten us about the pawnbroker murders of our own."

"*Da*," said the Russian with an exaggerated blink. "I met Detective Lestrade at Scotland Yard today after Museum trip. He invite me to office tomorrow to meet—what is word? —principals. Two English gentlemen and Russian informer. Most interesting. You gentlemen will be there also?"

"Yes," said my friend. "In fact, it was I who suggested to Lestrade that he collect the 'principals,' as you call them, for a round of questioning. At least two will not know who you are."

"Iss good," agreed the Russian. He was holding up the cigarette as he spoke, and I could not be sure whether he was referring to Holmes' plan or to his tobacco.

The three of us sat for some time in silence, the Russian puffing sedately, Holmes and I sipping our drinks.

When little remained of his cigarette, Porfiry Petrovitch crushed the stub in a nearby ashtray and rose to his feet. "Iss time to go," he said with a wink. "Tomorrow at Scotland Yard. Ten o'clock." Setting his top hat and side locks in place, he became once more a man of piety and exited our sitting room.

"Tomorrow should prove most interesting, Watson," said Holmes as he finished his drink. "I suggest you get some sleep." He then picked up his violin and announced, "I shall prepare for the encounter by immersing myself in Russian music—Tchaikovsky seems appropriate."

We climbed the stairs to our respective bedrooms, Holmes with fiddle in hand. As I fell into the arms of Morpheus, I found my descent accompanied by the heart-tugging cries and the lilting dances of Tchaikovsky's violin concerto.

Chapter Ten

Interrogations

Inspector Lestrade had reserved an interview room for late Saturday morning. Within it, two small, wooden tables abutted each other. On one side of the tables stood four chairs to accommodate himself, Porfiry Petrovitch, Holmes, and me. The single chair opposite awaited the subject to whom we would address our questions.

When Holmes and I arrived, Lestrade indicated where we were to sit. Minutes later, a uniformed constable escorted Porfiry Petrovitch into the room, and we all rose to greet him. Today, sans side locks, the Russian wore a traditional grey suit with matching waistcoat, and, blinking at us from across the table, leaned forward and shook our hands.

I must also add that during these salutations we were very much aware of an unexpected visitor who, exchanging words in Russian with Porfiry Petrovitch, had accompanied the detective into the room. This stranger wore a thick white beard, which thanks to its dramatic length, made him resemble some sort of Old Testament patriarch—a Moses, an Elijah, a Jeremiah. As he moved, a small crude cross of cypress-wood, which hung from his neck, would occasionally poke through the white tangles of beard reaching far down over his chest.

The stranger, dressed in brown trousers and coat, stood a few inches taller than the Russian detective. His short hair was darker and in greater abundance than that of Porfiry Petrovitch; yet the white beard, together with his penetrating but sad, tired eyes, made him look much older than the detective. The beard hid much of what obviously had once been strong, refined features, and one could easily surmise that in his younger years, this man had been quite handsome.

For his part, Lestrade showed none of the disdain he often displayed towards foreigners. In fact, revealing a respect for fellow law-enforcement officers that crosses international boundaries, the Inspector personally escorted the Russian detective to his place and provided an additional chair by the door for the bearded gentleman.

"*Horosho*," nodded the latter as he settled into the seat where for much of the session he would go unnoticed.

Minutes later, the same constable who had delivered Porfiry Petrovitch to us brought in the pale Roderick Cheek. Clad in well-worn jacket and trousers, the young man jerked his arm away each time the policeman, trying to guide him in the proper direction, touched an elbow. Finally, the vagabond plopped himself down onto the wooden chair that faced us. With all the rubbing at his nose and snuffling he displayed, it seemed clear that he had failed to rid himself of whatever illness continued to plague him.

Lestrade opened the session by identifying the two Russians in the room as police officials. The Inspector offered no names. Then he said, "A few questions regarding the late Mr Gottfried—if you don't mind, Mr Cheek."

Cheek nodded his compliance.

"Where were you and what were you doing Monday evening, the seventh of November of this year?" Lestrade asked. "It was the night of the two murders in Brick Lane."

Cheek emitted a sigh of exasperation. I had asked him the same questions. "Dunno exactly," he said slowly. "As I already told the doctor here, I was in my room, sick. Like now." He rubbed his nose again as if to prove his point. In fact, Cheek offered nothing different from the scant information I had got from him earlier.

Lestrade asked some inconsequential questions relating to how long Cheek had known Gottfried and how often Cheek visited the pawnbroker. Then he turned the interrogation over to Holmes. I was pleased to hear my friend echoing my own suspicions. "Mr Cheek," Holmes said, "please tell us what you know about the murders in Dostoevsky's *Crime and Punishment.*"

Porfiry Petrovitch, eyes blinking, had been looking round the room during much of Cheek's testimony. Now he focused his attention upon the witness.

As I have already written, Roderick Cheek had not been informed that sitting before him was the Russian detective who had overseen the investigation documented by Dostoevsky. In fact, Cheek had no reason to suspect that such an officer actually existed. Like virtually everyone else who had read *Crime and Punishment*, Cheek had no reason to discount the fictional nature of the Petersburg murders. Thus, as any educated literary person is trained to do, he summarised the events of the plot in the present tense. In Roderick Cheek, one could easily discern the student *manqué*.

"What do I know about the murders in *Crime and Punishment*?" repeated Cheek with a sniffle. "I know that Raskolnikov rehearses his crimes by paying an early visit to the pawnbroker. I know that once Raskolnikov learns that the pawnbroker's sister will be out of the flat at seven o'clock the next evening, he decides that will be the perfect time to kill the old lady—when she is alone. I know that before her murder he overhears someone else telling of the benefits of killing her. And I know that in preparation for the crime, he wraps a piece of wood in paper and ties it up securely so it can serve as a distraction.'

"And the killing itself?" Holmes prodded.

"Well, for the weapon, he borrows an axe from the nearby lodging of the caretaker and hangs it from the small cloth loop"—Mrs Garnett called it a "noose"—"which he has fashioned inside his coat for that purpose. When he gets to the old lady's flat, he gives her the tightly bound package; and whilst she fiddles with it, he whacks her from behind with the axe and crushes her skull. Then he does the same for her sister when she walks in on the crime. That's what I know." Between snuffles, he flashed a smile of triumph, the student flaunting his knowledge.

Lestrade seemed to consult his notes absent-mindedly. "Which end of the axe did he use," the policeman asked, his tone matter-of-fact, "the sharp end or the blunt end?"

To give Lestrade his due, only later would I realise that this was the singular question that Holmes wanted answered, the singular question which Cheek had been summoned to address. I gained no sense of the query's particular importance from the Inspector's passive expression. At the same time, however, the memory of thinking things not quite right at the Brick Lane murder scene began to emerge in my brain.

"For whose death?" Cheek asked in response to Lestrade's query, "the pawnbroker's or her sister's?"

"The pawnbroker's will suffice."

In spite of another sniffle, the young man smiled again. "Oh, the blunt end," he stated proudly. "Dostoevsky is quite clear on the matter. It contrasts with the coming attack on Lizaveta, the old lady's sister. She arrives unexpectedly and discovers the body whilst Raskolnikov is pilfering the jewellery. After she confronts him, he smashes her head in with the blade." Cheek concluded his report by drawing his sleeve across the bottom of his nose.

"Anything else, Mr Holmes?" Lestrade asked.

"I do have one final question for Mr Cheek," said my friend. "Do you own any books by Thomas Carlyle?"

Cheek furrowed his brow, as if considering the point of such a question. "Yeh," he finally answered. "The one on hero-worship."

Holmes nodded. "No further questions, Lestrade."

"We're done here then, Mr Cheek. That is, we're done here for *today*."

Lestrade called in the uniformed constable and instructed him to escort Cheek from the building.

"Take him out the back way," ordered the Inspector. "We don't want him conversing with his friend who's out there awaiting his own turn before us." Lestrade himself then left the room and returned with that very person.

Settling into the chair that Cheek had just vacated, William Arbuthnot lacked the resentment that characterised his friend. Indeed, clad in dark suit and waistcoat, he appeared to understand the gravity of the situation in which the two former school chums now found themselves.

Lestrade repeated to Arbuthnot the same questions the policeman had asked Cheek at the start—where was he and what was he doing on the night of the murders? —And he received equally unsatisfying answers.

"In my digs. Reading. For school." Arbuthnot also volunteered that he personally did not employ the pawn-broking services of Mr Gottfried and, in fact, knew of him only indirectly—through reports from Mr Cheek.

Then it was Holmes' turn to repeat his request concerning information about the murders in *Crime and Punishment*. Like Lestrade, he received virtually the same responses as offered by Cheek.

In the present tense, Arbuthnot reported Raskolnikov's plans, his execution of the crimes, his escape from the murder scene—just about everything Cheek had said save that Arbuthnot needed no prompting to describe the nature of the fatal attacks—that the first murder had been accomplished with the blunt end of the axe and that only the second had featured the sharp edge.

At the conclusion of Arbuthnot's questioning, Lestrade summoned the constable and had the young man escorted out in the same manner as Cheek before him. Once the door closed, Holmes exchanged looks with Porfiry Petrovitch. The Russian blinked and smiled, Holmes nodded at Lestrade, and the latter left the room to retrieve our third witness—the Russian informer I had previously met as "The Assistant."

Flat tweed cap in hand, he swaggered in, arms swinging, moustache tips still pointing dramatically outward. Yet he started when he recognised the Russian policeman staring up at him and stammered when he spoke his name: "P-Porfiry P-Petrovitch."

"Sit down!" commanded Lestrade.

The Assistant mumbled something in Russian. Then he lowered himself into the empty chair and placed his cap on the table.

"Ilya Petrovitch say he is surprised to see me." These were the first words in English that the Russian detective had voiced since entering the room, and he offered them with a dry chuckle. "He is not pleased. We left each other unhappy."

Holmes, Lestrade, and I all looked at the detective for further explanation.

"Poor fellow," Porfiry Petrovitch said, "always losing his temper. Many—how do you say? —nicknames—they tell story. In English—'Explosive,' 'Hot head.' Dostoevsky call him 'Lieutenant Gunpowder.' Too bad," the detective murmured, slowly shaking his head.

At Porfiry Petrovitch's feigned sadness, the Assistant clenched his fists. One could tell that he was seething.

"You know I saw notebooks of Dostoevsky," said the Russian detective to the rest of us on his side of the table. "In them are his plans for *Crime and Punishment*. Not all ideas appear in the book. Fyodor Mikhailovitch use many words besides nicknames to describe Assistant Superintendent. Difficult to translate into English, but I try." As the Russian listed the negatives, he counted them off on his fingers: "'base,' 'foul,' 'spiteful'—'scoundrel'." Looking directly at the Assistant, he said, "But you laugh at all this, Ilya Petrovitch."

Strangely, however, the Assistant was not even smiling. On the contrary, his lips had formed the straightest of lines, and his entire body seemed to tremble with anger.

"No need to tell you," the Russian detective went on, "we police knew this behavior of Ilya Petrovitch. For years, we saw him push citizens, shout at prisoners, scream at colleagues. But when he hollered at superior officer—that was—how do you English say? —'straw that broke horse's back.' I was that officer, and I sacked him—with approval, of course, from Nikodim Fomitch, our superintendent. Fomitch too called Ilya Petrovitch 'a keg of powder'."

Glaring at the Russian detective, the Assistant pointed his forefinger directly in the policeman's face. "I take confession in *your* biggest case. I take confession of Raskolnikov. He talk to *me*—not to *you*. Still, I, a proper man and a proper citizen, lose job. I get no money—not even for wife and children."

"So you came here," charged Lestrade, "and took the only position available to a disgraced officer—police informer."

At the word "informer," Holmes leaned forward. "Tell us what you remember of Raskolnikov's confession," he asked the Assistant.

Ilya Petrovitch twisted the right end of his pointed moustache. "Iss hard to remember. Iss twenty years since Raskolnikov come to me at station."

"Do give it a try," Holmes persisted.

The Assistant looked upward as he plumbed his memory. After a moment, he said, "Raskolnikov tell me he killed pawnbroker and sister with axe."

Almost immediately came Lestrade's seemingly harmless questions. "How did Raskolnikov describe the blows? Which end of the axe did he use?"

"He use blade on both."

Of course! Now I remembered what had seemed so strange at the scene of the murders. Cheek and Arbuthnot had correctly reported that in the novel the pawnbroker had been struck by the *blunt* end of the axe and that only her sister had been hit by the blade itself. "Hold on," said I, pointing out the anomaly. "Dostoevsky said that only *one* victim had been struck by the blade."

"Heh, heh, heh," cackled Porfiry Petrovitch. "Police try to keep secrets. I am sure you know, Doctor—innocent people confess. Remember house-painter Nikolay in book. After he confess, he try to hang himself. Who knows why they do this? Maybe religious Russians like Nikolay have need to suffer. It must be same in England. These confessors—they cannot know true facts—they were not there—heh, heh, heh— but still they confess. Iss why we want to hold back details. I tell untruth to Fyodor Mikhailovitch and newspapers—I say axe blade used for only *one* killing. Iss how we know who lies."

"Righto," said Lestrade with an appreciation of the Russian's professionalism. "We do the same."

Porfiry Petrovitch laughed again. "I say, we *want* to hold back details. We try. But Fyodor Mikhailovitch demand Truth. Wise man. He know I hide important facts. Complain. All the time, Dostoevsky complain. Finally, I tell him—blade used in *both* murders—but not to say in book."

"Wait a moment," cautioned Lestrade. It was only then that the logic of the whole business finally dawned on him. "Both Cheek and Arbuthnot knew about the events only as they were described in the Roosian book. They both agreed that the sharp edge killed *only* the pawnbroker's sister. In our murders, *both* victims were struck by the blade."

"Precisely," said Holmes. "That is why I asked the two young men to describe the crime as they knew it—that is, as Dostoevsky described it based on the *false* information Porfiry had fed him. Recall that most of the novel appeared in monthly instalments *before* Raskolnikov actually confessed. Apparently, once the killer was apprehended, Dostoevsky saw no need to correct the false information about the blades that he had already announced at the request of the police."

I could understand the author's thinking. Whether one or two wretches had been struck by the blade edge of the axe made no difference to his plot.

"But the police knew the *true* story," Holmes explained, "and when Ilya Petrovitch heard Raskolnikov confess to using the blade on *both* of the victims—not just the pawnbroker's sister—he knew Raskolnikov was telling the truth."

"Then," and here Lestrade cast his eyes on the police informer sitting across the table, "then the Assistant here—"

Suddenly, the man in question grabbed his cap, sprang to his feet and ran towards the door. He never made it through, however. For just as he reached for the doorknob, the white-bearded gentleman who had been sitting quietly near the exit all this time, extended his foot. The escaping Russian tripped right over it and fell flat on his face. The rumpus brought in the constable who had been positioned just outside.

"Grab that man!" shouted Lestrade, pointing at the fallen informer, "and bring him back to this chair."

As the constable wrestled the Russian into his seat, the man with the white beard rose and commanded our attention.

"Gentlemen," said Porfiry Petrovitch calmly, "may I present to you Mr Rodion Romanovitch Raskolnikov."

Chapter Eleven

Confessions

"I am Raskolnikov," the man announced in a thick Russian accent, "I am murderer Fyodor Mikhailovitch Dostoevsky wrote about." Pointing at the Assistant, he added, "I am man who confessed my crime to *him*."

"You—you are actually real?" I could not prevent myself from asking. Though I may have come to accept that Dostoevsky's murder plot was true, it still seemed hard to believe, even with the evidence quite literally standing before me.

"Da," he answered.

To spare the reader my inept recreation of Raskolnikov's broken English, I offer the following summary: For the murder of the pawnbroker and her sister, Raskolnikov was sentenced to ten years of hard labour in a frigid Siberian prison—two years longer than Dostoevsky had predicted in the epilogue to *Crime and Punishment*. As the novel reports, Sonia did follow him to Siberia and settle in a nearby village where she tended to him and to other prisoners as best she could. Dostoevsky accurately if ambiguously predicted Raskolnikov's future—what Whishaw translated as the man's "slow progressive regeneration"—when the narrator announced, "this may well form the theme of a new tale."

What we learned from Raskolnikov that day in Scotland Yard suggests the basis for that new tale, which Dostoevsky himself never reported. Released from prison after the allotted ten years, Raskolnikov remained exiled from St Petersburg. In spite of the cruel conditions in that part of the country, he married Sonia; and the two spent the next five years in Siberia, he working the barren fields, she taking in clothes for mending.

At the end of that period, the courts mercifully—and perhaps following the advice offered by Porfiry Petrovitch—granted Raskolnikov permission to return to St Petersburg. Happily, his old friend Razumihin, now married to Raskolnikov's sister Dounia, offered him a job in Razumihin's successful publishing firm. Raskolnikov requested a minor position—nothing too cerebral, nothing too demanding.

Reviving the linguistic skills he had employed in his former life, he devoted his time to translating German texts into Russian. Like Lazarus, to whom Raskolnikov never tired of comparing himself, he had been resurrected.

It was in Razumihin's publishing house that Porfiry Petrovitch found Raskolnikov—though the Russian detective had never really lost touch with the young man. As Porfiry Petrovitch had reassured him many times during their cat-and-mouse encounters, the policeman genuinely liked Raskolnikov. As a result, it did not require a great deal of persuasion to convince the reformed criminal to travel with the Russian detective to London. And why not—when the reason consisted of helping rid British society of a madman murdering people in the old style of Raskolnikov himself?

Once order had been restored in the room, Lestrade formally addressed Ilya Petrovitch: "Did you murder the pawnbroker called Samuel Gottfried and his wife Sarah Gottfried?"

The Assistant sat quietly. Though he had clearly tried to escape, as yet he had confessed to nothing. His face may have been turning red, but his only movement was an almost imperceptible drumming of his fingers on the wooden table.

"Was foolish idea," Porfiry Petrovitch said to the Assistant. "You were one of few who knew true details of killings in Petersburg. Not many suspects to hide among. Foolish to try to blame English people who do not know facts from twenty years past."

Lestrade snorted in amused agreement.

"Not smart," Porfiry Petrovitch charged, shaking his head once more. "I expect cleverness from Assistant Superintendent."

The more the Russian detective emphasised the poor planning of the murders in Brick Lane, the more the insolent Ilya Petrovitch seemed to fume.

"Long ago, you show wisdom," Porfiry Petrovitch resumed. "Today? *Tfu!*" The sound came out like an expectoration, and then the detective kept silent to let his disgust hover in the air.

The longer the silence lingered, the redder grew the Assistant's face.

Like the professional he was, Lestrade knew how long to allow the silence to continue. When he judged enough time had passed, he tried once more to pose the question: "I'll ask you again," said he. "Did you—"

"Da!" Ilya Petrovitch exploded, slamming his fist down on the table. *"Yes!"* he shouted. *"Yes!* I killed them. With axe."

No sooner did the Assistant begin his confession than Porfiry Petrovitch winked at Holmes. He had poked his quarry just hard enough. It was as my friend had said—the Russian detective well knew how to tap into the psychology of the criminal mind.

"I tell you why, Porfiry Petrovitch," the Assistant ranted, his English words tumbling out awkwardly, his voice dreadfully loud. "You sack me. I leave Russia, but wait long time for chance to prove my skill. To show you how smart I am. Years I wait. Finally, one day, I go to Gottfried with pledge; I meet Roderick Cheek. Student, no money, in debt to pawnbroker—perfect match for Raskolnikov. Perfect. I follow him. See where he live. Door always open. I steal Carlyle book. I can't read much English, but I see word 'hero'. Raskolnikov thought great men could commit murder and be free."

"On Cheek's well-stocked shelf," interjected Holmes, "I noted the space for a missing book."

"Like Raskolnikov, Cheek always ill." The Assistant allowed himself a disdainful chuckle. "Easy to blame Cheek for murders."

"But," said Holmes, "Raskolnikov considered *his* victim a leech, an oppressor, whose high rates were draining her poor clients. How could you kill an innocent man like Gottfried?"

"Was Jew," answered the Assistant with a shrug. *"Zhid."*

As if such foul reasoning explained anything at all.

"Like Raskolnikov," the Assistant went on, "I steal axe from caretaker, carry it in loop I sew in jacket. But Raskolnikov, he make mistake. After *I* kill Gottfried and wife, I throw axe into Thames—not try to put back like Raskolnikov. Stupid! And I throw jewellery into river. No clues—except book I leave in flat and small box with earrings I put on floor near stairs. I steal earrings from my wife when I leave Petersburg. I keep them for plan. Raskolnikov drop earrings—mistake; I leave box on purpose—part of plan, not accident. Ilya Petrovitch not foolish like Raskolnikov."

"Is that so?" said Lestrade. The bulldog in his soul was never more prominent than when he had the criminal in his grip. "I wouldn't accuse anyone of being foolish if I was you, Dmitry or Ilya or whatever it is that you're calling yourself these days. Mr Raskolnikov here served ten years. You'll swing for what *you* done." And Lestrade made a noose-like gesture, holding his fist to the side of his throat and pulling upward. To complete the sardonic tableau, he leaned his head to the side as if his neck had broken, popped his eyes wide open, and, gasping, stuck out his tongue.

The Assistant paled at the sight.

"Constable," Lestrade said once he regained his composure, "lock this man up. We'll fix the details later."

No sooner had the deflated Ilya Petrovitch been led from the room than Raskolnikov, leaning towards Porfiry Petrovitch, whispered something to him in Russian. The detective nodded and turned to us to explain.

"Vassia—iss nickname—reminded me of dream he had years ago. I tell Fyodor Mikhailovitch about it, and story appeared in novel. In dream, Vassia saw Ilya Petrovitch beating and kicking Vassia's landlady. She scream. Only a vision. But even in dream, Vassia knew the brutality of Assistant. Important dream—iss like Pushkin story, no?"

Unfortunately, I had no answer to his question. None of us did. But now I had another Russian author to read.

"We go back to Petersburg now?" Raskolnikov asked.

Both men turned to Lestrade for the answer.

"You men have served us quite well here," replied Lestrade. "And thanks to Mr Holmes, if we need your services again at the trial, we'll know how to get hold of you—though to be honest I don't think that will be necessary. The man's attempt to escape and his own confession should seal his fate."

Porfiry Petrovitch nodded. Then he turned to Raskolnikov and said some more words in Russian. I assumed them to be assurances that, after stopping in at their rooms in Montague Street, they would be taking the train to Queenborough and returning to St Petersburg.

Holmes had a final question. "Before you go, Porfiry Petrovitch, I must ask you to clear up the point I wondered about in Petersburg. Just before Raskolnikov confessed, you told him that you had clear evidence of his guilt. But according to Dostoevsky, you never explained to him what it was."

"Of course I did not say," agreed the Russian. "Otherwise Rodion Romanovitch might not surrender on his own."

"What was it?" Holmes asked. "What was this incontrovertible proof?"

"Heh, heh, heh," laughed the detective. "The proof? Poor Vassia think he is careful, but caretaker see him return axe. I have witness from the start. Case closed."

Reliving his foolishness, Raskolnikov sank his bearded chin into his chest. Porfiry Petrovitch draped a comforting arm round the man's shoulders as they headed toward the door.

Lestrade escorted the four of us to the kerb just beyond the entrance to the red-and-white-bricked police headquarters. In the shadows of the building, he extended a cordial farewell to the Russians. At the junction of Great Scotland Yard and Whitehall, Holmes flagged a passing hansom.

"*Do svidaniya*," both men said. "Good-bye," added Porfiry Petrovitch with a final blink of his eyes.

"Never knew Russkies could be so helpful," observed the policeman as we watched the waves of traffic swallow up the cab. Then he clasped his hands behind his back and returned to the building.

Holmes smiled for a brief moment before he and I set off on foot for Baker Street.

Chapter Twelve

A Final Word

At breakfast the next morning, I read aloud to Holmes the following story that appeared in the *Daily Chronicle*:

Inspector G. Lestrade of the Metropolitan Police announced yesterday the arrest of I.P. Poruchik, a Russian immigrant, for the murder of pawnbroker Samuel Gottfried and his wife Sarah. The crimes were committed in the couple's East End flat on 7 November. The murder weapon was a small axe. Such crimes are a hanging offence.

In an interesting turn of fate, twenty years ago, Poruchik, a former police assistant-superintendent in St Petersburg, Russia, took the confession of a similar axe murderer, whose wretched crime was the basis for a novel by the Russian author, F.M. Dostoevsky. According to Inspector Lestrade of Scotland Yard, the similarities were pointed out by Mr Sherlock Holmes, a private investigator.

"Bah!" I exploded, tossing the paper onto the table. "Not a word about *me,* the person who was first to link the murders to *Crime and Punishment.*"

"You have every right to be disappointed, old fellow," said Holmes, sipping his coffee. "But after working intimately with the Scotland Yarders long enough, you will discover that giving credit where credit is due is not one of their strong suits."

"I suppose you are right, Holmes. But they did give that credit to *you.*"

Holmes chuckled. "Yes, I suppose I should feel some sense of pride."

"Bah!" I said again, doubly frustrated by Holmes' reception of the honour that should have gone to me.

I was about to pick up my coffee when a knock on the door sounded.

"Enter!" commanded Holmes, and in marched Billy the page.

"Two gentlemen and a lady to see you, Mr Holmes," he announced.

"Show them in, Billy. I believe I know who they are."

Holmes and I both hurried to put on our coats whilst the three entered. As I too had anticipated, our guests turned out to be the twins, Priscilla and Roderick Cheek, as well as friend William Arbuthnot. Actually, since Miss Cheek's hand rested on Arbuthnot's arm, I suppose that "friend" was not the most accurate of terms.

Nor was this romance the only new development since our meeting at Scotland Yard just the day before. Though the dark circles beneath Roderick's eyes suggested lingering signs of illness, the young man had cleaned himself up most miraculously. His tangled, long hair had been trimmed and combed; his face was clean-shaven, and he now wore a grey-brown suit and waistcoat that gave him an altogether respectable appearance.

(In point of fact, I had seen Cheek's suit before. I recalled its colour being similar to that of an earthenware pot once held by the suit's true owner, Mr Arbuthnot. But the two men were of similar size, and the fit seemed close enough to minimise any criticism.)

"Mr Holmes," said Roderick with a cough, "we owe you a great deal." He was holding the same copy of the *Chronicle* that I had been reading.

"These murders have made me face reality," said Cheek, "and I didn't like what I saw."

Priscilla stepped forward and put her arm round her brother. "William and I are very proud of Roderick, Mr Holmes. He has told us of his plans to return to King's College and pursue the law. As you can see"—and here she fussed with her brother's hair—"he has already begun the process of reforming himself."

"Well done," said I as the young man blushed.

"Miss Cheek and I have made some plans as well," announced William Arbuthnot. "After she rid herself of that cad Percy Farragut, I was able to tell her my true feelings. We shall work out the financial challenges, and Roderick will begin tutoring young students again to offset some of the difficulty. As a result, gentlemen, I am happy to announce that once I complete my schooling, Miss Cheek has consented to become my wife."

"Well done!" I said once more—only this time with even greater enthusiasm. A story that started out so tragically seemed to be ending on quite the positive note.

"Watson speaks for me on all counts related to the human heart," Holmes said to our three guests, and I took some pleasure in finally gaining a degree of credit for my words.

"We must be off now," said Priscilla. "There is just enough money left in our inheritance to get Roderick back into school and to find him rooms in a less depressive environment than Goulston Street."

Holmes and I wished them well and watched the trio depart. The case had ended. No sooner had we returned to our coffees, however, than I found myself surveying a line of fiction books on the shelf behind the table.

"Holmes,' I mused, "do you know that there are countless murders in the works of Edgar Alan Poe?"

"Indeed. Why do you ask?"

"This Dostoevsky business makes me wonder if any of Poe's stories might inspire recreations. Perhaps I should be reading all of them just in case."

Holmes laughed. "First, s Russian writer, now Poe, an American—why not try someone home-grown, old fellow? I hear Charles Dickens left an unsolved murder or two worthy of investigation."

Why not indeed? I pondered as I brought the coffee to my lips once more. And yet even then I knew I was running in circles. For as long as there were criminals performing dastardly deeds and Sherlock Holmes to investigate their crimes, I well knew the nature of my future literary endeavours. And I told Holmes so.

"I suppose tomorrow will tell," said he.

Tomorrow! With all the excitement of completing the case of the murdered pawnbroker, I had completely forgotten that the next day—Monday, 21 November—would see the publication of *A Study in Scarlet.*

In just a few hours I hoped to be basking in the literary glow of my first published work. At the time, I did not know how it would be received. Still, I could always hope. If the reviews were encouraging and if my medical practice allowed me the opportunity, then—who knew? —I could easily fancy myself reporting a few more adventures of my friend and colleague, Mr Sherlock Holmes . . . .

THE END

The Editor's Suggestions for Further Reading

Although there are many different English translations of Fyodor Dostoyevsky's[10] *Crime and Punishment*, one should read Frederick Whishaw's translation (published by Courage Books) in order to recreate Dr Watson's experience. Dover Publications offers Constance Garnett's version, an excellent Audible recording of which is read by Constantine Gregory. A more modern translation has recently been done by Oliver Ready (published by Penguin Classics).

Dr Watson himself referred to an informative companion to the novel, Dostoyevsky's own *Notebooks for Crime and Punishment* (Dover Publications). Among the numerous collections of critical analyses of the novel, there are insightful articles in *The New Russian Dostoevsky* edited by Carol Apollonio as well those in Harold Bloom's two collections, both titled *Modern Critical Interpretations:*

---

[10] The more contemporary spelling of the author's name. (DDV)

Fyodor Dostoevsky's Crime and Punishment (Chelsea House, 1988, 2004).

Biographical accounts shedding additional light on the novel include Richard Garnett's biography of his grandmother, *Constance Garnett: A Heroic Life* (referred to by Watson in his Prologue) and Claudia Verhoven's treatment of the unsuccessful assassination attempt of Tsar Alexander II, *The Odd Man Karakozov: Imperial Russia, Modernity, and the Birth of Terrorism* (Cornell University Press).

Needless to say, *A Study in Scarlet*, Watson's heralded account of the first investigation he shared with Sherlock Holmes, was published on November 21, 1887. The rest, as they say, is history.

Also from Daniel D Victor

The American Literati Series

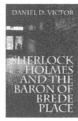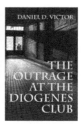

The Final Page of Baker Street
The Baron of Brede Place
Seventeen Minutes To Baker Street
The Outrage at The Diogenes Club

"The really amazing thing about this book is the author's ability to call up the 'essence' of both the Baker Street 'digs' of Holmes and Watson as well as that of the 'mean streets' of Marlowe's Los Angeles. Although none of the action takes place in either place, Holmes and Watson share a sense of camaraderie and self-confidence in facing threats and problems that also pervades many of the later tales in the Canon. Following their conversations and banter is a return to Edwardian England and its certainties and hope for the future. This is definitely the world before The Great War."
Philip K Jones

www.mxpublishing.com